Praise for
THE JOURNAL OF
ANTONIO MONTOYA

"A haunting story you will not soon forget, told in gifted style."
—Rudolfo Anaya

"Beautifully written . . . Collignon delivers his own engaging
brand of magical realism with a spare style, deadpan humor and
bracingly fresh descriptions."
—*Publishers Weekly*

"Graceful . . . quirky . . . inventive Southwestern surrealism."
—*The New York Times Book Review*

"A literary masterpiece . . . a memorable debut . . . told with
humor and compassion, *The Journal of Antonio Montoya* is
haunting, even hallucinatory, in its beauty."
—*Wisconsin Bookwatch*

"Strongly reminiscent of the magic realism of Garcia Marquez,
this is an enchanting work by a new writer."
—*Library Journal*

"Sensitive . . . lyrical . . . beautifully wrought . . a finely crafted
novel . . . a story of fantasy, reality, life, and death."
—KUVO Denver (NPR)

"A bountiful feast . . . a magical story told in a style at once
simple and sophisticated . . . a lovely and humorous examination
of the possibilities of realistic relationships with what has been
called the darker side . . . Thank goodness for books like Rick
Collignon's *The Journal of Antonio Montoya*."
—*Hobbs* (NM) *Daily News-Sun*

THE
JOURNAL
of
ANTONIO
MONTOYA

Rick Collignon

AVON BOOKS ◆ NEW YORK

AVON BOOKS
A division of
The Hearst Corporation
1350 Avenue of the Americas
New York, New York 10019

Copyright © 1996 by Rick Collignon
Front cover photograph by Charles Stirum
Inside back cover author photograph by Shana McTague
Published by arrangement with MacMurray & Beck, Inc.
Visit our website at http://www.AvonBooks.com
Library of Congress Catalog Card Number: 95-52618
ISBN: 0-380-73056-1

First Avon Books Trade Printing: October 1997

AVON TRADEMARK REG U S. PAT OFF AND IN OTHER COUNTRIES, MARCA REGISTRADA, HECHO EN U S.A.

Printed in the U.S.A.

OPM 10 9 8 7 6 5 4 3 2 1

To my wife, Julie,

And my children, Shana, Nick, and Ollie,

And to my mother and father, who gave me the love of words,

And maybe most of all to those who are the pages of this book.

O N E

José Montoya's mother and father were killed early one warm August morning by a cow.

José's father had once warned his son, when they were alone together in their trailer, that if he ever saw an owl he should watch out. José Sr. had drunk a few beers and was watching nothing on the television when he suddenly turned and told his son that owls were not birds, they were witches in disguise. They had no purpose but to bring news of death, his father had said, and if José were to see one around the house, he was to get the .22 from under the bed and kill the sonofabitch. José hadn't known what to say to his father. He had looked at him until his father turned away, took another drink from his beer, and said, "I tell you, hijo, those owls are something."

In his seven years José couldn't recall ever having seen an owl, and he knew that he hadn't seen one on the morning his mother and father died. The morning seemed to be just the beginning of another day and then, suddenly, without a cloud in the sky or the soft whisper of an owl's wing, it went bad. It went bad like a bloody egg his mother would sometimes crack open.

José's Tío Flavio drove his truck slowly through Guadalupe and took the dirt drive that angled sharply up the hill just past Felix's Café. He could see his brother's trailer at the top of the hill. The curtains were drawn over the windows and the front door was closed, even on such a warm morning. To Flavio, who liked trees and running water and the sound of things, the trailer, sitting on its patch of barren earth and surrounded by stunted sagebrush and the twisted shells of José's abandoned vehicles, looked like something that would be left after the end of the world.

Ray Pacheco, the Guadalupe police officer, had called Flavio with the bad news that his brother and his brother's wife, Loretta, were dead because of a cow. It had been over very quickly and no one had suffered, not even the stupid animal. The first thing to come into Flavio's head was, Why this morning? I was going to irrigate this morning. He had hung up the phone and said to his wife, "José and Loretta are dead. Call Ramona. I'm going to get little José."

He parked his truck in front of the trailer and stayed sitting in the cab. He thought it was too bad he had quit smoking—this would be a good time for a cigarette. He had quit because his wife, in her quiet way, had never approved of his ruining his health, but now, he thought, a cow had killed his brother, and after he got José from the trailer, he would go to Tito's bar and buy a carton of the cigarettes without filters.

Flavio walked up the front stoop to the trailer door. He swung the door open and then waited for his eyes to become accustomed to the shadows inside. He could hear the low sound of the television, and gradually he made out José sitting cross-legged in front of the TV, staring at him. Flavio had never been close to his brother's son.

He did not know why this was so, as little José was his only nephew, but whenever they were in each other's presence, Flavio would feel his thoughts slip from him, and when he did speak, the words sounded harsh and empty, even to himself. Flavio looked at his nephew for a few seconds and then said, "José."

José was still in his pajamas, and Flavio thought that his nephew must have just come from bed. "José," he said again, "go put on your clothes."

José stood up slowly and looked at his uncle. "Why, Tío?" he asked.

"Because your mother and your father were in a bad accident. We're going to my house."

"Was it a car accident?"

"Yes," Flavio said. "Now don't ask me no more. Go get your clothes and we'll go."

———————

José Sr. and Loretta Montoya drove to Las Sombras every Saturday morning. It was one of the things, José thought, that he did for his wife. He would get up early with Loretta, and with a splitting headache from too much beer the night before and a cigarette stuck in his mouth that tasted like dirt, he would climb into their car and drive the thirty miles south from Guadalupe to Las Sombras so Loretta could shop. She would hold her husband's hand tightly and drag him from shop to shop, tormenting him. But she never bought a thing, only walked and looked and sometimes touched the garments in the shops. Loretta had decided to make these trips each Saturday morning when, early in her marriage, she noticed that every Friday night José would get staggering drunk with his cabrónes and come home at all hours. On those nights, he would carry to her bed the odor of tobacco and beer and sweat that made Loretta think of car engines. Loretta shopped every Saturday morning for revenge.

On this particular Saturday morning Loretta had yelled at her son just before she and José Sr. had driven off. She seldom raised her voice to little José, but on this morning something had risen in her like a black bubble, and she had spit it out at her son. She'd stood in the doorway dressed in her tight blue jeans and fluffed white blouse with pictures on it of what she thought were armadillos but were actually turtles and had stared at José sitting in front of the television, a piece of uneaten toast beside him on the carpet. She had yelled his name so loudly that he started and looked at her wide-eyed. She didn't say anything else but turned and stomped down the steps to join her husband in the car. When José Sr. saw the expression on her face, he turned the radio off, tossed his cigarette out the window, and thought that his life might actually get worse.

A few miles south of Guadalupe, just as the highway topped a hill and began to fall back down sharply, Loretta began to cry. José, who was struggling to light another cigarette with a match that would not stay steady in his hand, reached over and touched her knee. His cigarette fell from his mouth to the floor of the car, and he grunted and bent over to look for it. Loretta, her eyes damp and now as bloodshot as her husband's, saw a large animal standing in the middle of the highway. Loretta could see the jaws of the animal moving back and forth calmly, and even as she called José's name, she saw that the animal was a large cow and that it had a look almost of curiosity in its eyes. By the time José straightened up, the front of the car had already struck the cow, knocking it off its four legs and rolling it through the windshield. José thought something had fallen from the sky. He saw the color black. He could smell the odor of grass.

TWO

IT RAINED THE DAY Loretta and José were buried. The sky the day before had gradually become streaked with white, and in the night the wind had stopped and the clouds had become thick and heavy and had banked up against the mountains. At dawn the day of the burial, rain had begun to fall lightly. A gift to his pastures, Flavio had thought. But by mid-morning the clouds had fallen to the base of the hills in shrouds, and the air had become water.

Loretta and José lay in their caskets in the mud at the edges of the two graves that had been dug side by side the previous day, when the earth had been hard and dry. Now the sound of the rain on the wood was so loud that Ramona had trouble making out the words of the priest. He spoke with his head bent, which made it worse, and it seemed to her as if he were mumbling on purpose.

The road leading up the hill to the cemetery was so slick that before leaving the church, they re-moved Loretta and José from the back of Father Leonardo's station wagon and placed them in the bed of Flavio's truck, where the pine boxes slid and bounced into each other on the ride up. One last time, Ramona thought. At the cemetery the footing was so treacherous that when they unloaded José from the back of the pickup, one of the pallbearers slipped and the casket fell on his foot. The man, a Friday-night compadre of José's of whom Loretta had never approved, remained to help carry both coffins to the edge of each grave and then limped painfully down the hill and got into his car and sat drinking whiskey by himself, watching how the rain fell. The mourners who remained huddled loosely together, not daring to lower the caskets into the holes for fear that the wet wood might slip on the rope, and who knew what would happen then?

Ramona stood in the mud and felt the rain fall upon her bare head and run down the back of her neck. The black dress she wore hung flatly from her hips, the wet fabric pressing against her thighs. Her boots were caked with adobe that had splattered to the hem of her dress. She wrapped her arms around her chest and hunched her shoulders and felt a chill run through her body.

It had been just two days since Ramona's brother and her brother's wife had died. Ramona had been washing paintbrushes at her kitchen sink and looking out the small, twisted window at how high the weeds had grown under the cottonwoods when she saw the ambulance pull out quickly from the village office. She wondered who had fallen dead from a bad heart. It wasn't until an hour later that Flavio's wife, Martha, called and said, "Your brother, José, is dead, and so is Loretta."

Since the death of her father, Ramona had made it a practice never to attend funerals. This had been fine when she lived elsewhere, but since her return to Guadalupe, it seemed as if someone were always dying, and if she hadn't known the deceased, she had known their first cousin or their in-laws or some other relative. The act of ignoring funerals, not to mention marriages, baptisms, and church gatherings, had gradually made people feel as if Ramona Montoya were someone who had moved into their midst from the outside. This was a constant embarrassment to Flavio, who thought it his duty to say good-bye to all of Guadalupe's dead regardless of how much he disliked them. Once, when Flavio had reprimanded Ramona for not observing community protocol, she had stared at him in stony silence until he left, leaving her alone in the house that had been their grandparents'. He never broached the subject again with his sister, and now a part of him was astonished that she had actually attended the burial of their brother.

Few people had come to the cemetery, and those who had stood about as miserably as Ramona. No one had thought to bring an umbrella. In fact, no one in Guadalupe owned an umbrella. When it rained, you stayed inside. No one was foolish enough to go outside and stand in it.

Father Leonardo finished speaking and laid his hands on the lids of both coffins. He raised his head and smiled and asked if anyone wished to speak. Flavio raised his hand slowly as if he were still in school, and when the priest nodded, he said, "My brother would not want us to catch pneumonia." After he spoke, Flavio thought that he really didn't know what his brother would have wanted, and in all honesty, if anyone were foolish enough to stand stupidly in the rain, it possibly would have been José.

Father Leonardo nodded and said, "Es verdad, Flavio." He stretched out his arms and blessed the small gathering one last time and then turned and walked away quickly. Ramona followed the line of people, and after a few steps, she took a moment to glance over her shoulder at where the coffins sat. She felt her body turn to ice. She felt as if her heart had stopped and there was no more breath in her body. Loretta was sitting up in her casket, her blouse wet and molded to her breasts. Her head was cocked a little bit, and she was running her fingers through her hair, threading out the rain.

"It is not a very good day to be buried, Ramona," she said. "In the mud. I hate the mud. How your brother would track it through the

house like he was blind. Always making a mess."
Loretta shook her head, and Ramona could see
drops of water fly from her black hair.

"Loretta," Ramona said.

"Ramona," Loretta said, "I have something to
ask of you."

"Loretta," Ramona said again, although she
wasn't sure she spoke aloud.

Loretta dropped her hands down to where
her lap would be. She leaned her body toward
Ramona. "Ramona," she said, "I want you to take
little José. I don't want him to be with my family.
And I don't want him to be with Flavio and
Martha. I want you to take him, Ramona. Do this
for me.

"Loretta," Ramona said again, "You shouldn't
be talking to me."

Loretta smiled, and Ramona could see her
youth. "What should I be doing, Ramona?"

Behind Ramona, Flavio had climbed into his
truck. He rubbed his hands together, thinking no
one should feel this cold in August. He looked out
the windshield at his sister. She was turned away

from him so that all he could see was the back of her body. He could see her head move slightly every so often, and he wondered what she was doing still standing in the rain. He turned the key in the ignition and flipped on the heater switch. He wished Ramona would hurry so he could get home and drink a cup of coffee and smoke some cigarettes.

Ramona did not know what to say to Loretta. She could hear the engine of Flavio's truck turn and then start. She thought that this conversation with her sister-in-law had gone on long enough. "I must go," she said.

"Promise me," Loretta said, still with a smile.

"I'm not a young woman," Ramona said. The ice that had gripped her body had receded, but now she could feel the dampness of her clothes against her skin, a warm feeling in her head like a fever. Even the thought of a seven-year-old boy made her feel like there was no blood in her body.

Loretta waved her hand gently at her and shook her head. "I don't want to sit in the rain forever, Ramona." And when Ramona didn't answer, Loretta said, "Thank you." She lay back down in her casket, letting her body fall softly.

"Loretta," Ramona whispered.

Loretta raised her head above the edge of the pine box. "Yes, Ramona."

"I don't understand any of this."

Loretta made a slight shrugging motion. "How could you, Ramona?" she said. "You will get sick standing in the rain."

Ramona and Flavio drove from the cemetery in silence, not speaking even when the truck slid out of the ruts going down the steep hill and Flavio had to take his foot off the brake and pray the vehicle would pull back. When they made it safely to the highway, Flavio breathed a sigh of relief and glanced at his sister. Ramona was staring out her side window, watching the rain run like a small creek down the side of the road. Flavio looked back out the windshield. He wondered how he could have a sister so different from himself. Between them, even "good morning" seemed difficult. He thought of his brother and Loretta and then of how he would have to go to their trailer soon and board up the windows and shut off the gas and empty the refrigerator before things began to spoil. The idea of cleaning out the food from his brother's house made Flavio feel sadder than he had at the news of their deaths.

Ramona leaned against the door on her side of the truck with her cheek pressed against the damp glass. She stared blankly out the window and felt the heater splay hot air on her knees. She sat there feeling tired and empty and old.

Ramona remembered when her mother had died of a strange illness that had caused her arms and legs to go numb, a numbness that spread rapidly to her heart. Ramona had stood in the Guadalupe graveyard and looked at her grieving father and her brother Flavio, who was eleven with the mind of a tree, and at her baby brother, José, who although three years old could only walk backward. Ramona, at nineteen, could suddenly see the rest of her life. That night she packed a small suitcase, and the following morning, she left town on the bus that stopped every day at Felix's

Café. Thirteen years later, after the death of her grandfather, Ramona had returned to Guadalupe on what she could swear was the same bus.

Flavio pulled off the highway just past Felix's Café and turned onto a gravel road that followed the creek as it wound through the valley. He drove past his fields and saw how green the alfalfa had become with just the morning rain. He hoped it would rain forever, or at least until it was time for him to cut the fields once last time before autumn. After a mile or so, he turned off the road onto his drive, long and narrow and thickly lined with apple trees.

The house had been their father's, and it was where Flavio and Ramona and José Sr. had spent their childhood. Their father had built it with his own hands early in his marriage. After his death, Flavio had waited a brief time and then moved into the house, giving his brother a great deal of the furniture and a beige cast-iron cookstove that at this moment was rusting in the rain behind José's trailer. To Ramona, he had given their mother's wedding ring and the chickens and turkeys that had lived in a shed behind the house.

After the death of their mother and after Ramona's departure from Guadalupe, their father, who had always liked the taste of whiskey, began drinking in earnest. Blessed with a strong body and a mind that stayed calm even on windy days, he was able to consume vast amounts of alcohol and still hold his job at the copper mine. Flavio remembered his father during those years in much the way that one remembers a wall. Five years after Ramona returned to Guadalupe, their father dropped dead in Tito's bar one afternoon while reaching into his pocket for change. The medical examiner in Las Sombras told Ramona and Flavio and José Sr. that their father's heart had shrunk to the size of a large marble and was the color of old snow. The burial of her father eight years ago was the last funeral Ramona had attended, and at least, Ramona thought, her father had had the decency not to sit up in his coffin and converse with her.

The wake for Loretta and José was being held at the home of Loretta's parents, so the only vehicles in Flavio's drive were his wife's car and, beside it, Ramona's pickup. Flavio pulled in next to the truck and parked. He shut off the engine and sat listening to the sound of the rain on the cab. He hoped that the tar he had spread around the base of his stovepipe last spring was keeping out the water. He looked over at Ramona and cleared his throat. When Ramona looked back at him, Flavio could suddenly see that his sister was aging. Lines like feathers branched away from her eyes, and there may have been more gray than black in her hair. Her eyes were red with a darkness below them, and Flavio was reminded of his mother when she would lie ill in bed and hold her arms out to him. She would say softly, "Mi hijo, come here to me." Flavio suddenly felt sad again, and when Ramona spoke, the sound of her voice startled him.

"Flavio," she said.

"Yes," Flavio said too loudly.

"Is little José here, or is he at his abuela's?"

"José is in the house," Flavio said. "We're to go over to Loretta's family."

Ramona grunted. She pushed the truck door open, climbed out of the cab, and with long strides walked to the house. Flavio sat in the pickup for a moment watching his sister, and then he got out and trudged after her through the mud.

Flavio's wife, Martha, was in her kitchen wrapping the tortillas she had made in a warm towel. She had begun cooking the moment she received news of Loretta and José's death. On the counter about her were platters of enchiladas in a sauce of thick red chile. Stacks of pork tamales that she had wrapped in cornhusks. Posole and menudo and chicharrónes. There was a bowl the size of a basin full to the brim with salsa with so much cilantro in it that it was the first thing Ramona smelled when she entered the house. José was standing at the side of the sink, cutting garlic that Martha would sprinkle over the enchiladas, when Ramona walked into the kitchen.

"Hello Martha," Ramona said. "Hello José."

Martha was a small, round woman who was at a loss as to what to say to nearly everyone. She knew she was this way because of her mother, who was also small and round, but who had been born

mute and so never said anything to anyone.
Martha had adored her sister-in-law, Loretta, for
the simple reason that Loretta could talk and talk
without any need of a response. When the two of
them were together, Martha spoke only to prod
Loretta into another long monologue, and then
she would go on with what she was doing and listen to her sister-in-law as if the words Loretta
spoke were woven with poetry. With Ramona, it
was different. Ramona seldom spoke, and the si-
lences that fell between them made Martha con-
stantly uncomfortable in Ramona's presence. Oddly
enough, Ramona had always admired Martha and
often wondered how her brother had come to
marry a wife who cooked so well and kept the
house neat and was never angry. When Martha saw
Ramona enter the kitchen, she prayed that her
husband would come soon.

"It rained," Martha said, laying more tortillas
on a towel.

"Yes," Ramona said. "The mud was everywhere." José had stopped what he was doing and
was staring at her. Ramona could see Loretta's

wide eyes in his face and the darkness of his skin that had come from the Montoyas. "José," she said softly, reaching out to touch his shoulder, "please go get your coat." When he had left the room, she turned to Martha.

"Loretta spoke with me once, and she told me that if anything ever happened to her and my brother, I was to take little José."

Martha turned to Ramona and felt that her mouth had opened. She closed it and tried to smile. She heard the front door open and the sound of her husband's boots coming toward the kitchen.

Flavio walked through the living room and came a few steps into the kitchen. "Flavio," Martha said, "Ramona is here."

"Of course Ramona is here," he said. "She came with me." He felt awkward and irritable. He wished his sister would leave so he could feel comfortable in his own house. "Are you ready to go?" he asked his wife. "Yes," Martha said, "in a moment," and she went to the stove and took two towels from the oven that she had placed there to warm. She went back to the counter and draped the towels over the three stacks of tortillas.

"José," Flavio yelled. "Get your coat. It is almost time to go."

"Are his things here?" Ramona asked her sister-in-law.

Martha realized there were two different conversations going on among three people about the same thing. She thought, not for the first time, how fortunate her mother was merely to listen good-naturedly and not be placed in such positions.

"There's a bag in the living room," Martha said to Ramona. "Everything else is still in the trailer."

Ramona turned her head toward Flavio. "Maybe tomorrow you can bring the rest of his things."

Flavio had no idea what his sister was talking about. It wasn't until the front door closed a few minutes later that his wife told him Ramona had taken little José.

Neither Ramona nor José said a word as Ramona drove back to her house. José watched the rain and thought of the time when he was very little and had been outside his house during a lightning storm. His father had burst from the trailer and had grabbed him roughly around the waist and carried him inside. When his father put him down, he hit José hard on the butt and, with his face twisted in anger and fear, told his son to never again be outside during a lightning storm. There was evil in it. It would mess around all day up high, but when you weren't looking—and here his father had slashed his hand through the air between them—it would strike as quickly as the snakes at the river and boil the blood in your body. José's father had stood there breathing hard, and then he took a cigarette from his shirt pocket and lit it. He let the smoke out of his lungs slowly and then reached down and touched his son's arm. "Let's me and you have a soda, José," he had said. "We can watch the storm from inside."

When Ramona turned off the dirt road onto the highway, José began to cry silently. Ramona looked at him out of the corner of her eye and thought that this had been a foolish idea. She should turn the truck around and return José to

Flavio and Martha, who would care for him properly. Maybe it was true that Loretta had come back from the grave to ask a favor of Ramona, but it wasn't necessarily true that just because Loretta was dead, she knew any better.

Ramona drove through town and took the road behind the village office and pulled up to the front of her house. She shut off the engine and looked at her nephew. She would feed José some lunch, and then she would see. José looked over at her, and Ramona reached out her hand and brushed lightly at his hair.

"Let's go inside, José," she said. "We'll have some lunch and drink something warm."

The two of them climbed out of the truck. A slight breeze blew, and the water from the cottonwoods fell on them in large fat drops. Before they reached the house, the front door swung open and Ramona's grandfather, Epolito Montoya, who had been dead for thirteen years, stood in the doorway. "Why are you out in the rain?" he said.

THREE

RAMONA MONTOYA LIVED IN her grandfather's old adobe behind the village office in Guadalupe. It was a small house with a sagging pitched roof and five dark rooms that were slowly caving in on themselves. The white plaster walls inside had cracks the size of miniature chasms that ran, in some places, from the smoke-stained vigas almost to the floor. The window frames had all twisted out of square and looked out on the world at odd angles. The wood floors seemed to be closer to the ceilings than they had just a few years ago, and Ramona, at forty-four, was quite sure it wasn't because she was growing. She knew in her heart that her grandfather's house was turning back to dirt.

Ramona had lived for the past twelve years in her grandfather's adobe. She lived in this house

because when Epolito Montoya had died, just four
days after the death of his wife, Rosa, he had left
the house and his pasture and his pickup truck to
Ramona. He had left his chickens and his geese and
his three lambs to Flavio, and to José Sr. he had left
one acre of dry land that sat on top of a hill.
Epolito had done things this way because of all his
grandchildren, Ramona was his favorite. José Sr., as
a young boy, would visit only when forced to and
even then would sit in the house and twitch his
body and stare out the small windows so much that
Epolito would have preferred the boy hadn't both-
ered to come at all. He left José the one acre of dry
land where the wind blew because he knew that
when José stood there, his grandfather would not
be far from his thoughts. To Flavio he left his
lambs and chickens and geese because as a child,
Flavio had once thrown a rock and killed his wife's
favorite cock, which had been named Pierre.

Ramona became her grandparents' favorite the
year she was seven and lived with her grandparents
while her mother and father and baby Flavio jour-
neyed through Utah in search of work. Epolito

had always thought of that year as the sweetest in his life. Ramona had been a shy girl and seldom left his wife's side. In the kitchen, they would cook chile together and mend and, at Christmas, bake biscochitos. When Epolito came into the house at dark, his granddaughter, with her braided black hair and her large dark eyes, would sit beside him at the table and eat in silence. After eating, Epolito would sit in the living room, and he would some-times hear his wife scold Ramona in hushed tones, and then he would hear the sound of Ramona trying to hide her laughter. His wife would say, "Hush, Ramona, you are too loud. You'll disturb your grandfather." Epolito loved his granddaughter in the way one loves something that he can never have.

Ramona and little José sat at the small table in the kitchen while Ramona's grandmother served them beans and chile and a fresh sopapilla each. Epolito was in the living room, sitting in the stuffed chair that looked out the window at the village office and, beyond that, the rain-drenched Sangre de Cristo Mountains.

When Ramona and José had entered the kitchen, Ramona's grandmother had been on her hands and knees scraping a spot of dried paint from the floor with the edge of a knife. Epolito had said, "Look at your abuela like that. You weren't raised to throw your paints around our house like this," and then he had grunted and turned and walked out of the room. Ramona and her grandmother had looked at each other until, finally, her grandmother had smiled and asked if they were hungry.

Ramona ate slowly and watched her grandmother straighten up around the sink, her back humped slightly in the shoulders, her long hair gray and knotted in the back. To Ramona, her grandmother looked exactly the way she had forever.

"Grandmother," Ramona said, "what are you doing here?"

Rosa Montoya wiped her hands on her apron and turned from the sink. "You always had a loud voice, Ramona," she said. "You don't want to disturb your grandfather." She walked over to the table and stood next to José. She placed her hand on José's head and moved it through his hair.

"You're such a big boy, hijo," she said. "And smart too, I think." José could feel her hand cold from the sink water on his scalp. He looked up at her.

"Have you always been here?" he asked.

"No, hijo, your grandfather and I have been away. But never too far away." She looked at Ramona and smiled. Ramona could see that she was wearing her false teeth. Rosa looked back at José. "Do you think that if we were always here we would hide from such a boy as you?" Ramona heard her grandfather cough in the other room, then a groanlike noise as he rose from the chair and walked to the window.

"I thought you were dead," José said.

"I am a little bit dead," Rosa said. Ramona watched José nod and then take a bite from his sopapilla as if what his great-grandmother had said made perfect sense. "Take that into the other room, José," Rosa said, "and go visit with your grand-father. And be careful, hijo, not to make a mess."

José pushed away from the table and walked out of the kitchen. Ramona heard her grandfather say his name and then the soft sound of José's voice. Her grandmother sat down across from her. "There's no food in this house," she said.

"It's been just me," Ramona told her.

"That's no matter. There's a child now who needs to eat. And what if you had guests? And where are your babies?"

"I'm too old for babies, Grandmother."

"You were going to marry that nice Trujillo boy."

"That was nearly thirty years ago, Grandmother," Ramona said. She suddenly wanted her grandmother to leave her house. She did not want to talk about things she had forgotten. She did not want to sit in her kitchen and talk any longer to an old woman who had been buried years before. "Besides," Ramona said, "this is what I wanted for my life."

"What? To sit alone by yourself in this house? To do nothing but paint those stupid pictures?"

"You've seen my pictures?"

Ramona had begun to draw as a child. She drew, with sharpened crayons on lined paper, pictures of all the saints. Saints lost on dusty, abandoned roads, dressed in robes that fell from their necks to their bare feet. Saints lost in deep arroyos or wandering through thick piñon and juniper forests. She drew six saints stranded atop a boulder in a rocky canyon, all of them crowded together, with startled eyes. Ramona drew saints as if the world were populated with them, and they were always in the wrong place.

When Ramona grew a little older, she abandoned the saints and began to draw pictures of the people in Guadalupe as she thought they would appear naked. One day when Ramona was out of the house, Flavio crept into her room. He found under her bed a stack of drawings and spent a long time staring at the nude body of Horacio Medina, who was an old man and owned many head of cattle in Guadalupe. The picture under Horacio Medina was of Ramona herself. She was lying on her side, facing out, and Flavio could see her small breasts and the darkness between her legs. Flavio's eyes widened in shock, and he felt his forehead grow hot. He put the drawings back where they had been, and after that, when passing the door to his sister's room, he would stare at the floor and think of other things.

Ramona had always thought that when she grew up she would be a great artist. She would live in New York City and in the winter take trips to Europe. She would paint cathedrals and fields of wheat. She would paint the sky over distant places and the brick streets of unknown cities. She would paint the sound of the wind over the hills of Spain. And when she was dead for a hundred years, her pictures would be in books and the marks of her brushes would still speak.

When Ramona left Guadalupe after the death of her mother, she found that merely to exist was a difficult chore. She worked menial jobs that were always the same and met men who passed through her life as if they were no more than shadows. Through it all, she drew. She enrolled in art classes held late at night, and she sketched bowls of fruit and tired nudes, and she studied Picasso. Oddly enough, it was the art classes that gradually reduced her pencils to silence and made her feel that what she drew on her paper was of no worth. She didn't draw for three years; then one day she picked up a brush and began to paint the village of Guadalupe. She painted the outside of the Guadalupe lumberyard in the heat of summer and Felix's Café before dawn. She painted fields of sagebrush as the sun was setting bloodlike on the mountains. She painted trucks abandoned in arroyos in the midst of stunted piñon, and shovels spaded in the earth along irrigation ditches. She painted the Guadalupe church with its roof that swayed and bellied and its buttresses that grew from the ground and melded with the thick walls. Ramona painted the village of Guadalupe as if it lived in her bones, as if she and the village were haunted.

She thought of these paintings as her "village period" and was surprised when they began to sell. She had tried often to break away from putting on canvas the place where she had been raised and which she thought too ordinary, but whenever she began to work, Guadalupe seemed to appear again and again. Her "village period" had now gone on for nineteen years.

"How have you seen my paintings?" Ramona asked her grandmother again. The rain had finally stopped, and there was no noise in the kitchen other than the easy rasping of her grandmother's breath. A sliver of sun came through the kitchen window and filled the sink.

"How does anybody see things, Ramona?" Rosa said. "The shed is full to the ceiling with your paintings. You paint this village as if it were dead."

Ramona thought that of all people, her grandmother should have been the last person to make a statement like that. She also thought that what her grandmother said was true.

"I'm going to lie down now," Rosa said. "You should get out of those wet clothes." She stood up slowly. It seemed to Ramona that her grandmother wasn't much taller than the chair in which she had been sitting.

"You're going to stay here?" Ramona said.

"This is our house. Where else would we stay?" Rosa walked around the table and stood behind her granddaughter. She touched her lips to

Ramona's hair. "For dinner," she said, "we will have enchiladas."

Ramona stayed sitting in the kitchen. In the silence she could hear her grandfather's voice from the other room.

"When I was young," Epolito said, "there wasn't no mine here. There was nothing. Just the village. And the people. We kept our cows up high in the mountains in the summer, and before the first snow, we'd bring them back down for winter. If you needed something, you got it from your neighbor or went to the priest or to the man who kept the village records. Maybe you'd go to Las Sombras once or two times in a year. Sometimes in the spring to get seed, or in the summer when there was fiesta. People don't know anything anymore. They get their paychecks from the mine, and they don't care about nothing else. They buy whatever stupid thing comes into their mind. They sell their father's land to these tourists for a few dollars, and what do they have? Nothing. A new pickup that breaks in a year."

"We went to fiesta once," José said. "My mother wouldn't let my father drive on the way back, and when we got home she threw rocks at him."

Epolito grunted, and Ramona could hear the springs in the chair as he moved his body. "Your father could never sit still when he was a boy. He was like one of those little dogs that always run around barking at the wind. Your mother should have hit him in the head with one of those stones."

Actually, Loretta had hit him in the head. One of the rocks struck José Sr. in the forehead hard enough to make him stagger backward and fall down hard on his butt. He had sat there with his legs splayed and his mouth open, blood running down his face and dripping off his chin onto his pants. José was standing on the trailer steps next to his mother, and he thought that she had killed his father. After a few seconds of silence, Loretta let out a little squeal and hurried over and helped her husband to his feet and into the house. She cleaned his face with a damp rag while José Sr. mumbled about his stupidity. Later, after getting José Sr. to lie down, Loretta sat by herself in the living room and stared out the window for a long time.

"José," Epolito said. "Instead of walking in circles, go into the kitchen and get a chair. I don't know why your Tía Ramona has only one chair in here anyway."

Ramona watched José walk into the kitchen. He looked at her and said, "Grandfather wants me to bring a chair."

"That's fine, José," Ramona said.

He came to the table and picked up the chair their grandmother had been sitting in. "Tía," José said softly, "what does a little bit dead mean?"

Ramona looked at him for a moment. He was a thin boy, not so tall, with black hair that needed cutting. He looked like any other boy to her. "I don't know what it means, José," she said.

"Do you think since Grandmother and Grandfather are here that my mom might come?"

Ramona saw Loretta sitting up in her coffin, threading the rain from her hair. Ramona thought that if she wasn't being haunted, it was possible a part of her had always been blind. She smiled slightly. "And what about your father?"

"My father too."

"I don't think so," Ramona said.

"But you're not sure?"

"What I'm sure of, José, is that your grandfather would like you to be with him. Go visit with him."

José turned and went into the other room, and Ramona heard her grandfather say, "Here, José. Put it next to me."

Ramona remembered the year she lived with her grandparents. She had been in the first grade at the elementary school, and although the school was no more than a mile away, her grandfather made her ride the school bus that stopped out on the highway. Each morning, she would leave the house with her grandfather, who would walk a few feet behind her all the way to the bus stop. There, he would stand by himself with his hands deep in his pockets, staring off at the mountains. He never spoke to the other children, who kept their distance, and Ramona would stand awkwardly between them and her grandfather as if caught between two worlds. When the bus arrived, he would always exchange a few words with the driver, and Ramona, as the bus pulled away, would look out the window at her grandfather, his head bent, walking home. In the winter, she could see his breath.

"Look at how green the mountains are, José," her grandfather said in the living room. "Even after so little rain."

Instinctively, Ramona looked out the kitchen window. She could see the leaves of the cotton-woods still dripping water. The sky between the branches was blue. She could hear the sound of birds.

There was only silence from the living room for a long time, and when Ramona finally roused herself from the chair, she walked to the sink and washed her face over and over with warm water. She felt exhausted, and after drying her face, she stood for a moment staring out the small window. She pushed the glass open and could feel the breeze on her face and the smell of wet earth. A truck started up across the road and pulled out of the village office, its tires caked with mud. Ramona took a few deep breaths and walked quietly into the other room. Her grandfather was asleep in the chair, his chin down on his chest, a rumbling noise coming from his open mouth. José had dozed off too, his body bent sideways, the side of his face resting against the arm of the stuffed chair. José's eyes opened, and for a second he looked at his aunt before the eyelids fluttered and closed. Ramona looked into her own bedroom and saw that her grandmother had chosen to lie down there. She rested far to one side of the bed with her hands folded neatly over her breasts.

Ramona went into the last room of the house, where there was a small cot. She lay down in her clothes and covered herself with a thin blanket. She stared at the water-stained vigas, at the clods of dried adobe between the latillas that still dropped dirt when the wind blew hard. When Ramona thought of ghosts, and since her childhood this was seldom, she always thought of La Llorona.

As a child, Ramona, like every other child in Guadalupe, had been told the tale of La Llorona a thousand times. La Llorona, who in life had drowned her own children, walks the creekbeds and arroyos and ditches and wherever else there is water, calling out for her lost children. Since the entire village of Guadalupe was criss-crossed with irrigation ditches, to be out after dark was an uncommon risk. La Llorona could be anywhere: in the call of an owl, in the coyote's shrill bark, or in the water as it flowed from field to field.

The year Ramona turned nine, she saw La Llorona. She was certain of the age even now because it had also been the year that Emilio Silva, an old man who lived by himself next to Ramona's parents, had been seen by his neighbors chasing after his chickens with a torch he had welded together. He had caught many of them, and his flock had scattered, running into the road and into Ramona's yard with burnt, smoldering feathers and an expression of the apocalypse in their small red eyes. Emilio later told his neighbors that he had done such a thing because at night, when trying to sleep, he could hear his chickens talking to each other and was unhappy at what they had to say. It had been the autumn of that year, and Ramona and her mother and her father and little Flavio had gone into the foothills to pick piñon. It was there that Ramona had seen La Llorona. She was standing beneath a tall pine tree that grew by itself at the upper edge of a large open meadow. From where Ramona had stood, she could see how black and long La Llorona's hair was and how her dress, which was startling white, fell from her neck to her ankles. Ramona had watched this woman watch her for a long time, and when her parents had returned from the woods with a bag heavy with piñon and Flavio held sideways in her father's arm, she had asked her mother who the woman beneath the tree was. Her mother had looked and seen nothing, and with an uneasy expression on her face, she had gathered their things and they had left the hills quickly.

When Ramona thought of ghosts, she thought of La Llorona: a lost soul who walked the hills and creeks in search of children. She certainly did not think of her grandparents or her sister-in-law, Loretta. She was not uneasy in their presence, but their being there made her feel as though her life hadn't moved. Her grandparents had returned home as though they had never left, and Ramona wondered if they would ask her when she was leaving. She thought that the idea of death was to let the living go on, not to have to eat enchiladas with one's dead relatives.

Ramona woke with her heart beating rapidly and the heavy sound of silence in the house. She felt disoriented from sleeping in a room she seldom used, and for a moment, she had absolutely no idea where she was. She lay on the cot for a little while, letting her heart calm and her memory return. When Ramona was as composed as she thought she would become under the circumstances, she sat up and swung her legs off the cot. She rubbed her eyes and brushed her hair back from her face. She thought that with her black dress now quite wrinkled and her hair tangled about her face, she must look like a witch.

The living room was empty, and in the kitchen Ramona found her grandmother peeling green chiles at the sink and crying. There was the smell of onions and garlic and lard.

"There's some coffee, Ramona," Rosa said, not turning from the sink.

"What's wrong, Grandmother?" Ramona asked.

"Nothing, hija. I get sad sometimes. It's nothing to worry. I've become like the weather." She turned on the tap and rinsed a chile. Ramona could never remember seeing her grandmother cry. She'd been a woman who'd always kept moving.

"Take some coffee, Ramona," Rosa said, "and go sit down somewhere. This has been a hard day for us all."

Ramona poured a cup from the pot. "Where is José?" she asked.

"He's out walking with your grandfather."

Ramona leaned back against the counter. She took a drink of coffee and felt a coffee ground on her tongue. She didn't want to think about what José and her grandfather taking a walk might mean. She put her cup down. "Let me help you," she said.

"No," Rosa said without looking at her grand-daughter. "You go somewhere else now. I can do this by myself."

Ramona picked up her cup of coffee and went outside. She sat in an old wicker chair under the large cottonwood. It was late afternoon, and in the hours Ramona had slept the sun had dried up much of the moisture from the morning rain. The sun was still high in the west, but where Ramona sat she was shaded by the branches of the tree. She could feel the high grass on the calf of her leg and hear water running in the irrigation ditch that ran along the edge of her property near the road.

Across the road, Ramona could see the back of the village office, a new building that had been constructed just a few years ago. Off to the side of the village office was an old adobe that was en-gulfed in weeds and abandoned machinery. The roof of the building sagged in the center, and even from so far away, Ramona could see how bloated and caked with tar the roof was. She noticed that the one door stood open, and she thought that the interior must be full of skunks and bats and should probably be locked up so that children wouldn't wander in.

Ramona had painted the building a few months ago. She had sat alone in her kitchen, as she always did, with her paints and a white canvas and closed her eyes for a long time. And then, for no particular reason, the old adobe had come to her. When she finally picked up her brush, she began to make indecipherable gestures that eventually resolved into the slanted frame of one of the windows in the adobe. She had worked in a frenzy and completed the painting by midafternoon. Much of it resembled her other paintings, something caught as if in a photograph of things that no longer lived. But there was something else in this one. She had caught a whisper of life with her brush, as if the painting wished to speak, and none of the words would be Ramona's. Unfortunately, Ramona had no idea how she had done this. She put the picture with the others in the shed where her grandfather had once kept his chickens and his geese.

Ramona brought her cup to her mouth and watched Flavio's truck pull off the highway and

onto the dirt road that ran between her house and
the village office. He drove slowly by and parked
beside Ramona's pickup. Ramona watched her
brother climb out of the cab and wondered how,
with the same blood in their veins, they could be
so different. Where she was tall with legs that were
long and slender, Flavio was short and slightly
bow-legged. It was as if their father had jumped a
fence and brought back one of them from somewhere else. The only way in which Ramona
thought they might be alike was that they both
tended to be quiet and spoke with reticence. But
even then, Ramona had always thought that her
brother shared this trait with her only because his
brain was the size of a small stone.

Ramona watched Flavio walk across the boards
that she had laid over the irrigation ditch, and she
saw that her brother was beginning to put on
weight. He walked toward her with his eyes staring
down at his feet. When he stopped, just a few
paces from where Ramona was sitting, he looked
past her at the house. Flavio could see where the
plaster had pulled away from the wall in places and

how the wood was rotting beneath the window frames. He could smell the sweet odor of chile and garlic.

"Hello Flavio," Ramona said.

Flavio looked sideways at his sister. "Ramona," he said, "I came to take little José."

Ramona emptied her coffee on the ground between them. "Take José where?" she asked.

Flavio coughed and cleared his throat. After Martha had told him that Ramona had taken José home to live with her, he had driven to Loretta's parents' house, still in a state of shock. At one point, while he was drinking a beer and eating a pork tamale, Loretta's mother had approached him and with her two hands clasped to her full breasts, she had asked, "What will become of little José?" Fulfilling Ramona's notion regarding the size of his brain, Flavio had answered, "Don't ask me. Ramona has taken him." Silence followed this statement, which seemed to have been heard by everyone in the room. Loretta's relatives wanted to know what Flavio's sister, who had never married and did nothing but paint her pictures and who lived amongst them like a stranger, was going to do with a child. Flavio had answered with a variety of shrugs and facial expressions that had told no one anything. When he finally felt he could leave the wake without being noticed, he drove Martha home and then went straight to Ramona's. He thought that what he was trying to do was ward off certain disaster, but he was also curious about just what had possessed his sister to take José.

"I think it would be better," Flavio said, "if little José was around other children."

"You don't have children," Ramona said. This was not where Flavio wanted the conversation to go. His and Martha's lack of children had always been a torment and a mystery to him. Both had wished for children from the moment Father Leonardo had clapped his hands together in mock delight and pronounced them man and wife so many years ago. After three years of marriage and more sexual encounters with Flavio than she thought humanly possible, Martha had come to the conclusion that she had inherited her mother's muteness in her womb. She drove to Las Sombras alone one day to see a woman who knew of such things, and the woman told her that there was nothing wrong with her, that the fault must lie with her husband. Not knowing how to tell Flavio this news, she had placed the results of the tests in Flavio's lunch box, where he found it after feeding his cows at noon.

When he returned home that evening, he placed the papers on the table and asked his wife just what it was he had found with his tamales. Embarrassed, Martha told him that her female organs were fine and that she was sorry. Pleased that his wife was well, Flavio didn't grasp until a few days later just what it was she was sorry about. Months later, Flavio, alone, drove to Las Sombras, where a young doctor did a sperm count for him and pronounced him a complete man with enough lively sperm to populate a small South American country. For a year after that, Flavio and Martha, in the darkness of their bedroom, made love in so many different manners that Martha would sometimes find herself blushing even when alone in her kitchen cooking. And yet, nothing happened. Flavio had finally reached the sad conclusion that his and Martha's insides must be like acid and base, like rain on snow. Something died when his sperm swam inside his wife.

"Ramona," Flavio said, "I didn't mean for José to live with me." Which was true. Flavio had now spent so many years alone with his wife that the thought of a child made him uncomfortable. Flavio reached in his shirt pocket and took out a cigarette. He lit it and inhaled the smoke deep into his lungs. "There are other relatives," he said to his sister. "On Loretta's side."

Behind Flavio, across the road, Ramona saw two figures walk out of the abandoned building beside the village office. One was a stout man of medium height, and the other was small and thin and was carrying something in both his hands. The two walked slowly across the field toward Ramona's house, and she could now see that it was her grandfather and José. She looked up at Flavio and thought that he smoked his cigarette the way a woman in a city might.

"Flavio," she said, "this has been a difficult day. And I know that you mean well." From inside the house came the clatter of a pan falling to the floor.

Flavio looked toward the house. "What is José doing in there?" he said. He looked back at his sister, who was staring past him. Flavio turned his head and saw José approaching the road before Ramona's drive. He could also see that a few yards behind José was an old man. Flavio thought there was something familiar about this man.

"Do you see him?" Ramona said in a whisper. "Tell me, Flavio, that you see him."

"Who?" Flavio said. "José or that viejo?" Flavio squinted his eyes. "Who is that?" he said, and for the first time all day, which seemed to have lasted forever, Ramona felt something heavy lift from her. She leaned back in her chair and found herself smiling.

José ran across the road. "Tío," he said. "Hello, Tío." Flavio ignored his nephew and continued staring at the old man, who had just reached the far side of the road. I know that old man, he thought.

"Tía," José said, "we found this."

In José's hands was a book. Ramona could smell mildew and saw the water stains on the cover and how the cloth had been chewed by rodents. She thought that it must be covered with bat droppings.

"Why are you carrying that, José?" she said. "It's covered with filth. Take it inside, but keep it out of the kitchen. And wash your hands. Wash them twice."

"Tell Grandfather," José said, and he half walked, half ran past Ramona and went inside the house. Ramona could hear the sound of her grandmother's voice.

Flavio hadn't taken his eyes off the old man. Grandfather, he thought. Qué grandfather? The old man crossed the road slowly, looking both ways a number of times as if he could no longer trust his own eyes. He was wearing a baseball cap pulled low, and Flavio saw that he favored one leg slightly. The old man was close enough now that Flavio could see the set of his mouth and how he tapped one hand against his thigh as he walked. Flavio felt the blood in his veins stop flowing.

Epolito stopped a few yards away from Ramona and Flavio. Flavio and his grandfather were of the same height, and Ramona noticed how her grandfather's legs seemed to bow out at the knees, as did her brother's.

"Are you rested, hija?" Epolito said to Ramona.

Ramona felt her smile grow and thought she might laugh aloud. "Yes," she said. "I am, Grandfather."

Epolito looked at Flavio. "You look well, Flavio," Epolito said. "Ramona, you make sure your brother doesn't throw any rocks. I don't want any more dead chickens."

After Epolito walked by Flavio and went into the house, Flavio stood openmouthed and pale, staring straight ahead as if he had seen a ghost— which he had. When the door to the house slammed shut, Ramona saw Flavio's shoulders jerk, and she thought that if her brother did not run to his truck and drive away, it was possible he would fall to the ground in a faint. Instead, he turned his body and looked down at his sister.

"Ramona," he said harshly, "how can this be?"

"Grandmother's in the house," she said to him. "She's cooking enchiladas."

Flavio felt his mind slide toward darkness. He remembered that when he was a small child first learning to read, no matter how hard he tried to concentrate, the letters would sit on the page stealing his thoughts from him. He knew that his mouth had dropped open, and that he was breathing too fast, and that his sister must think that he looked like a dog on a hot day.

Ramona rose from her chair and took her brother's arm. "Flavio," she said, "sit here in the chair."

"Ramona," Flavio said.

"I know, Flavio. Our grandparents have come back."

Flavio took in a deep halting breath of air and let it out slowly. "I think I better go," he said. At this moment, the door to the house opened. In the doorway stood Rosa Montoya, small and thin and gray, with the front of her apron wet and stained with chile.

"Flavio," she called out with delight, "you will stay for dinner."

Flavio didn't say a word. He stood frozen, his eyes blinking rapidly. When he finally opened his mouth, Ramona heard him say in a whisper, "Grandmother."

"He has to go home, Grandmother," Ramona said. "To get Martha. He'll come back later." Flavio nodded his head up and down slowly in agreement.

"Bueno," Rosa said. "Come soon, hijo." With that, she turned and disappeared inside.

Flavio backed away from his sister and then turned and walked to his truck. Ramona watched him climb behind the wheel, and without a glance behind him, he backed into the road and drove off.

FOUR

R AMONA, JOSÉ, AND THEIR GRANDPARENTS ate
together at the small table in the kitchen. Rosa
had the kitchen door open, and Ramona could feel the
breeze take the heat from the stove out of the room.
Through the open door, Ramona could see one wall of
the shed behind the house, where she stored her paintings. The old wire that had once kept in chickens was
twisted with weeds and stepped down in places. A few
hours of daylight remained, and Ramona felt that this
had been the longest day of her life.

"What did Flavio say?" Epolito asked. He spoke
with food in his mouth, his jaws working, his eyes
looking down at the plate.

"He came to talk about José," Ramona said.
She watched her grandfather move a tortilla
around his plate with his left hand.

"Talk what about me?"

"Don't talk with food in your mouth, José," Rosa said.

José was sitting next to his grandfather, and Ramona could see how Epolito's elbow touched José's shoulder. She watched José chew the food in his mouth and then swallow. She looked at her grandfather and wondered how it was that a face as smooth and dark as José's would someday become like that of her grandfather, gray and heavy.

"Your Tío Flavio thinks you should live somewhere else," Epolito said. "He thinks you would be better off with your mother's family."

"Did you know, José," Rosa said, "that your mother's grandmother, her name was Guadalupita García, was born with horns?"

Both Ramona and José looked at their grandmother. "It's true," she went on. "There were tiny bumps under her hair, one on each side of her head, and if you gave Guadalupita something she wanted she would let you touch them. Her parents tried to keep it quiet that their daughter was born with antlers, but Guadalupita had a big mouth and would tell everyone. She thought that this was something to be happy about. A lot of the Garcías, especially back then, were like that. You wouldn't want to live with people whose ancestors were born with horns, would you, hijo?" Rosa slid the plate of tortillas toward José. "Eat, hijo," she said. "You're too skinny. The wind will blow you."

José took a tortilla from the plate. "My mother's grandmother was like an elk?" he said.

"Almost," Rosa said.

"But my mother wasn't like that," José said.

"Oh no, hijo," Rosa said, and she reached over and placed her hand over José's. "Your mother was a beautiful woman. And hardworking. Like you, who will grow up and always be proud of her."

"The problem with Flavio," Epolito said, "is he never worries about what he should. He worries about things that have no meaning. Did he think when he picked up that rock that it could kill a chicken? No. And then he thinks up a lie only a fool would believe. That a chicken would fly down from a tree at just the moment he threw the stone. Who does Flavio think I am to believe such a story?"

"The breeze feels good, doesn't it, hija?" Rosa said to Ramona.

Ramona looked at her grandmother, and after a moment she smiled and said, "Yes, Grandmother, it does." She thought that if she shut her eyes, she would be like a child again.

Epolito scraped his chair back from the table. "I'm going to let the water on the field," he said. He looked at his granddaughter. "It has been dry for too many years."

José grabbed another tortilla and stood beside his grandfather. "Can I help you?"

Epolito grunted, and Ramona watched the two of them walk out the kitchen door. She heard Epolito say, "Get the shovel, José. It's there by the shed."

Rosa rose and began clearing the table. When Ramona began to help, her grandmother told her to sit back down. She went into the living room and returned with the book José had brought into the house.

"Your grandfather brought this for you to look at," she said. She placed it on a small dishtowel before Ramona. "You sit and I'll make us some coffee, Ramona."

Ramona looked down at the book. Again, she could smell the strong odor of mildew. The thick cover was bloated and warped and chewed around the edges. She could see the date, 1924, printed in ink and faded on the cover. She wondered if it was possible to catch something mortal from the filth on the book. Carefully, with her fingertips, she opened the cover to the first page.

It was a journal, the entries written in Spanish, the handwriting small and cramped. There was but one line on the first page, and it read, "Un otro año." Ramona turned the page and there was nothing. It wasn't until January 27 that she found another entry. Ramona looked up at her grandmother, who was at the sink. "What is this, Grandmother?" she asked.

"Read, hija. You always have so many questions."

JANUARY 27:
*There is a bad pneumonia. Fires burn in the cemetery
to thaw the ground, and today I helped dig the graves
for the infant of Juan and Leonardra Mondragón
and also for Delfino Rael, who, according to his wife,
Stella, was sixty-seven years of age and in good
health until he fell ill six days ago. The weather
remains cold and wet, and I believe that is why
so many are ill. There are five of our village who
have died since Christmas. I write this late in the evening,
and I do not have the will to work on the Lady. Of
late, I have kept this journal poorly, and as this is the
story of this village, I pledge that from this date it will
go better.*

Ramona looked up from the book. There was a
cup of coffee on the table before her. Her grandmother was no longer in the room, and Ramona
realized she hadn't heard her leave. Ramona took
a sip from the cup and turned the page.

JANUARY 28:

It snowed in the night. From where I sit, I can see the village. There is smoke coming from all the chimneys that hangs over the village like a shroud. I can see that Horacio Medina's cows have once again broken through their fence and now stand down the hill from this office in the middle of the road. I can count twelve cows, and the snow is midway up their legs. Their tracks and those of Father Joseph leading from the door of the church are the only marks in the snow.

JANUARY 29:

This morning, Father Joseph came to this office in boots not made for this season to say that Lydia García's fever had abated in the night and that she would recover soon. And also, he told me, the snow had extinguished the fires in the night, and possibly this was a sign from God. He asked me how the new santo was progressing, and I told him that with all the digging, there was little time for such work. We sat quietly after that, and as he left, he told me that sometimes it is difficult to keep one's faith and one's sense of humor. I agreed with these words. It is evening now, and I write this in my kitchen. Today, at noon, the sun broke through the

*clouds, and for the first time in so long I could feel warmth
in the air.*

JANUARY 30:

*Miguel Romero, the son of Manuel and Cora Romero, was
standing in the snow outside the office waiting for me when
I arrived. The sun had not yet risen above the mountains to
the east, and the air was cold. Miguel is a tall, thin boy of
thirteen, and if he stood straight, his eyes would be level with
mine. He told me his father wished to speak with me before
there was bloodshed. We walked to his house, which sits in
the valley and is not far from the creek. Horacio Medina's
cows were still standing in the road, and as we passed,
Miguel struck one with a ball of snow in the center of the
forehead. When we arrived at Miguel's home, his father,
Manuel, a small man much shorter than his son, was outside standing in the cold with his hands in his pockets. I
asked Manuel what was wrong, and he looked away from
me at the mountains, which are covered with more snow
than I remember ever seeing before. He said that he was
sorry that his family had disturbed me but that his wife,
Cora, wished for him to shoot his neighbor, Gustavo
Ortega, and that if he didn't, his wife had said that some*

night when everyone was asleep, she would take the rifle and shoot Gustavo herself. When I asked how this had come about, Manuel kicked at the snow with his boots and said nothing. At that moment, Cora Romero opened the door of the house. She is a large woman and wide, with thin legs. She said that I should come into her house and out of the cold but that her husband could not.

Cora told me her neighbor, Gustavo Ortega, an old man who has lived alone since the death of his wife, had offended her by telling her youngest son that his mother was so fat that if she were a cow she could feed the village through the winter. This had been said seven days before and had not disturbed Cora until this morning, when she woke feeling poorly and told her husband that if he did not shoot Gustavo, she would.

Cora gave me coffee. I told her that this had been a long and hard winter and that pneumonia had been especially bad this year and that even now spring was far. When I finished, I told her that what Gustavo had said was insulting and of no purpose and that I would speak to him about this.

Gustavo greeted Manuel and myself at his door. When he invited us inside, I said no and told him that we had

come to speak with him about Manuel's wife, Cora.
Gustavo, whom I know to be in his seventies and suffering
from loss of sight so severe that his right eye is the color of
milk, stepped out from the house and asked what it was he
could do. I told him that Cora had heard of what he had
said about her and that she felt bad about this. Gustavo looked
down at the frozen earth and moved his feet, which were
clothed only in heavy stockings. I told him I had come so
that there would be no trouble and that I thought with all
the illness this winter that this was all very foolish. Gustavo
looked past me at Manuel and apologized. He said that he
had been thinking of his own wife that morning and of his
children, who had abandoned him by moving to the south side
of the village, and also that he had been drunk. Manuel nodded
and said that he would tell his wife this and that the winter
had been exceptionally hard and that it wasn't good for the
soul to be confined indoors for so long. I ate eggs and chile
with Manuel and his family and walked back to my office
alone. By late afternoon the sun had shrunk the snow almost
six inches.

Tonight I worked on the Lady. Her hand comes from
the wood, and I can see the flesh of her fingers.

Ramona looked up from the book and found herself staring blankly straight ahead. She could see out the kitchen door and noticed that the light outside had grown dull. The sun had fallen behind the hills to the west. She looked back down at the open book and read the last line once more. "Her hand comes from the wood, and I can see the flesh of her fingers." She wondered what it was she was reading. She saw how small and tight the handwriting was and thought that the man who wrote this must have labored over each word. Ramona let her hand rest on the open page for a moment and then rose from her chair and walked to the door. Across the field, she could see her grandfather bent over, working the shovel in the irrigation ditch. Beside him was little José, hands in his pockets, watching his grandfather work. Above the two of them was a sky at dusk streaked a soft red that echoed off the field and piñon hills and made the hills look full and lush. Ramona thought she had never seen anything so beautiful.

Ramona's grandmother had gone to bed while Ramona had been reading in the kitchen, and when her grandfather came into the house from the field, he washed at the sink and without a word retired into the bedroom, closing the door after him. Ramona and José sat quietly together for a little while in the kitchen until Ramona told him that it was getting late and he should lie down.

Ramona thought she would sleep in the chair in the living room. But after an hour of turning her body, she gave up and went into the room where José was sleeping. In the darkness, she saw a figure standing beside the cot. Ramona thought of La Llorona, and she felt her knees weaken and her heart race.

"It's only me," the figure said in Loretta's voice. "I just came to watch."

Ramona leaned against the frame of the door. She waited for her breathing to calm and then said in a whisper, "Did he see you?"

"No," Loretta said. She stayed by the bed a moment longer and then turned to Ramona. "I would like to hold him, Ramona," she said.

"Yes," Ramona said. "I know."

"It would not be good, would it?"

"No," Ramona said. "I don't think so," and for a little while the two women were quiet. "Loretta," Ramona said, "where is my brother?"

"Big José? He was always so slow, Ramona. You should know that. You are his sister."

"I feel like there is nothing I know any longer, Loretta. People who should not be here appear when they wish and for no reason. I don't understand any of this."

Loretta stepped closer to Ramona, and Ramona could smell the scent of cloves. "I came to see the length of José's eyelashes," she said, "and how his face looks when he sleeps. To hear his breathing. I came to look at his hands, which, by the way, Ramona, are too dirty. You have to make him wash before bed or he will turn into a little animal."

Ramona closed her eyes in the darkness. She thought that there must be the right words to say to her sister-in-law, but she had no idea what they were. When she spoke to Loretta she felt as though her words were no more than air. "Loretta," she said, "why is this happening?" When there was no answer, Ramona opened her eyes. Loretta was gone.

Ramona stood next to the cot in much the way that Loretta had, and after a while she undid the buttons in the back of her dress and let it fall to the floor. She bent over and gently pushed José to one side of the cot and crawled in beside him. She covered herself with the thin blanket. She could feel his leg warm against hers and smell the odor of mud on his skin. José turned toward her in his sleep, and she could feel his breath on her shoulder.

FIVE

RAMONA DREAMED IN THE NIGHT. She dreamed that the cemetery was on fire, and upon waking, she lay still, trying to grasp each image of this dream before it faded. She remembered quite clearly that she had seen the cemetery as if from a hill above it. She remembered flames sprouting from each wooden cross like blossoms until the fires joined together and the graveyard where Loretta and José and Ramona's parents and grandparents and all the dead of Guadalupe were buried became one mass of flames, the smoke black and churning just above the fire. Ramona couldn't remember any more of this dream. She became aware of José asleep beside her and realized that she had enough problems as it was. If her sleeping mind wanted to play games, it could do so without her participation.

José was lying on the cot with his back to Ramona, his face close to the wall. He had awakened briefly before dawn, his eyes open wide as if they had never closed. He had remained motionless and looked toward his Tía Ramona, who lay beside him. He then moved his body enough that Ramona stirred in her sleep and spoke to herself, and when José could feel the length of her body against his, he closed his eyes and slept.

Now, only moments later, Ramona slid carefully out of the cot and, still in her slip, went to the living room, where she could see into her grandparents' bedroom. The room was empty. The bed was neatly made, and light—not yet with sun—was coming in through the small, crooked window. Ramona took a pair of clean blue jeans and a white blouse from her dresser and went into the bathroom. She stood under the shower for a long time before she dried herself slowly and dressed. She stared at herself in the mirror while brushing her hair. Although wrinkles crowded the corners of her eyes, the rest of her face was smooth and clear and dark. Her hair fell unevenly to her shoulders, and there was maybe more white than black, and it came in streaks as if painted in. Putting the brush down, she leaned closer to the mirror. She thought she looked good for a woman of middle age who had spent the last twenty-four hours in confusion. After a moment, she raised her eyebrows slightly, and then she smiled at herself.

In the kitchen, a pot of coffee had been made, and on the table was a note. It read: "Ramona, your grandfather and I have gone for a ride. Make sure, if we are not back, that José eats well. There is coffee. Your grandmother, Rosa."

Ramona walked into the living room. She looked out the window and saw that the sun was still an hour away from rising above the mountains. She saw that the sky was a soft blue and that there was no wind. She also saw that her truck was gone.

Ramona poured a cup of coffee and sat down at the kitchen table. The journal was where she had left it the night before. She slid it close to her and turned the page.

JANUARY 31:

It is the last day of this month, and the temperature during the day rose above freezing. With his tractor, Filemon Rodríguez plowed snow from the houses where many of the older people live and also the road through the center of town. The sun melted much of the snow where he had plowed, and I could see dirt that hopefully will not yet turn to mud. Late in the day Filemon came to my office, and I paid him three dollars of village money for his work. We talked, both of us happy to see the end of this month. Just before dark, Horacio Medina came for his cows.

FEBRUARY 3:

The children returned to school on this morning for the first day since Christmas. Lito, the only son of Epolito and Rosa Montoya, joined me, as he often has, on the way from his house, which sits just west of the village office. We walked together, with Lito walking ahead of me. He is a small boy with clipped hair and a face that is open and round and not serious. His father is my first cousin, and although I can see Epolito in the boy's face, it is his mother I can see in his eyes, which are dark and seem to look everywhere. I asked

him about his father and his mother, and he did not answer.
When I asked once more, he turned and, still walking, said
that he had been drawing pictures of fish and wondered if
they had legs could they walk. After a moment, I told him
that I had never before seen a fish that grew legs, but that if
they did, it was possible they would walk everywhere. Lito
agreed. There would be fish in the alfalfa fields, he said, and
in the mountains, and if they had claws for their toes, they
would climb trees. I told him that this was something he
should discuss with his father, and he said that he had, and
Epolito had told him if fish had legs they would use them to
swim. I watched Lito walk down the hill, and two times
he fell. Each time he rose, he would run. In his hands he
carried a tablet.

Ramona stopped reading and stared at the page
until the words became a blur. The journal, until
now, had amused her. She had read as if reading
about a distant and familiar place. To have her
grandparents and the boy, Lito, who drew pictures
of fish and who was her father, appear on the page
was like a blow to her heart.

Ramona's memory of her father was not altogether pleasant. He had drunk too much, always, his drinking becoming even worse after the death of his wife. When Ramona thought of him, which was seldom, she remembered the smell of whiskey and stale tobacco and an expression on his face that was always somewhat baffled. Much of the time, her father did not return home until late in the evening, when his children were already long in bed, and when he did come home early, he had often been drinking heavily and would sit alone in the kitchen as if lost in his own house. He was not the father Ramona would have chosen, even if he had had the good grace to not be ill tempered.

Ramona recalled a time just after Flavio's birth when her mother had fallen ill with a disease that affected her eyes and caused her to see only the shadow of things. Her father had driven his wife and baby Flavio to the hospital in Las Sombras. When he returned, he was alone and told Ramona that her mother would soon be well but that she would be gone for a while. Ramona, who always felt shy and awkward when near her father, had then spent five endless days with him.

One morning, she had awakened later than usual. She wandered into the kitchen, still in her nightgown, and saw her father outside chopping wood. It was early November, and that morning had been cold with small flakes of snow falling. The clouds were low and thick on the mountains, and to Ramona it seemed that all there was to the world was this valley. She watched her father swing the ax again and again, the pile of split wood growing. She could feel the cold from the floor on her bare feet. Her father swung the ax hard and then let it remain stuck in the stump of wood. He lowered himself and crouched down on the balls of his feet. Ramona watched him bring his hands to his face. She saw that he was breathing hard and that there was snow in his hair. When he finally took his hands away, his eyes met Ramona's, startling them both. Ramona, in the kitchen, took a step back, and then her father smiled, almost shyly, and gently waved his hand. Ramona lifted her arm slowly, embarrassed, but not quite high enough for her father to see.

Sitting in her own kitchen thirty-seven years later, seven years after the death of the round-faced Lito, Ramona began to cry. She hiccuped and wept, and a part of her that was watching all this felt as if she were in the current of a river that was slowly pulling her downstream.

Little José chose that moment to climb out of bed and walk through the living room and into the kitchen. He saw his aunt weeping quietly at the kitchen table and thought that it would be better if he went back into the other room. Ramona raised her head, and José could see that her face was wet and swollen and that her lips seemed to be bigger than before.

"José," Ramona said in a voice that sounded like a cough. "José," she said again, more clearly, "where are your clothes?"

José was wearing his pajamas, which had blue stripes. He waved his arm behind him. "I'll go get them," he said.

"Not the ones from yesterday," Ramona said. "Clean clothes."

José stared at her for a moment as if she were speaking in a language with which he was unfamiliar. Finally he shrugged his shoulders and said, "I don't have any clothes." He spoke in a voice that suddenly began to waver, and Ramona thought that he too might begin to weep.

Ramona grunted loudly and then rose from her chair and went to the sink. She splashed cold water on her face and then looked out the small window. The sun had finally risen, and the shadows looked cool beneath the cottonwoods. She took in a deep breath of air and let it out in a soft hum. She turned and looked at her nephew.

"Come, José," she said, "let's eat."

Ramona brought him a large box of cereal and a half gallon of milk. She also brought a loaf of bread and jam and the platter of enchiladas left over from the night before. "There," she said.

"This is a lot of food, Tía," José said.

"Yes," Ramona said, "because you are a growing boy. And I want you to eat all of it."

José looked up at his aunt, who was standing near the table with her arms folded across her chest. She was smiling slightly. "I don't eat this much usually," he said. "I just eat cereal."

"Cereal is like eating air," Ramona said. "But if you eat two bowls, maybe that would be enough."

"Is there sugar?"

"There's sugar in the cereal," Ramona said.

"It's better with a little more."

"There's sugar in the cereal," Ramona said again, and José decided that he would be quiet. "Two bowls, José," Ramona said. "I'm going to call your Tío Flavio and see about your clothes."

On her way into the living room, Ramona heard the phone ring. When she picked it up, the voice on the other end said in a whisper, "Ramona, it's me, Flavio. Are they still there?"

"Where are José's things?" Ramona said.

"What?" Flavio said. "What things?"

"His clothes."

For a moment, Flavio was silent. Suddenly an awful fear went through him, and then he said, "Which José?"

Ramona closed her eyes and shook her head. Slowly and clearly she said to her brother, "Little José. That José. Your nephew. You were to bring his clothes yesterday."

Flavio thought that his sister had lost her mind. She was speaking in angry tones about a change of clothing when the dead were roaming her house. To placate her, he said, "Yes, yes, I'll get them. I'll bring them by this morning. Now, what of our grandparents?"

"They're not here, Flavio," Ramona said to him, and she heard the line go empty.

Finally Flavio said, "You mean they were never there?"

Ramona wondered at the brain that was inside her brother's head. "No, Flavio," she said, "that is not what I meant. They were here, but now they are gone."

"They're gone," Flavio echoed, and he felt a surge of relief.

"Yes," Ramona said, and then, without trying to hide the smile in her voice, she said, "They've borrowed my truck and are out taking a ride."

———————————————————

After Ramona hung up the phone, Flavio stood in his own kitchen with the receiver still in his hand. Martha was standing at the sink with her back to her husband, washing the dishes. She had heard the conversation between Flavio and Ramona. The evening before, when Flavio had returned home in a state of shock and told Martha that his grandparents had returned from beyond the grave to haunt him, Martha hadn't known how to respond. The thought that her husband, whom she loved dearly, had suddenly gone insane crept into her mind, and then she chased the thought away and smiled and went to the counter and baked cookies until late in the evening. Now, after hearing the talk between Flavio and his sister, Martha thought she would wrap tamales in corn-husks and make tortillas for the remainder of the day.

Flavio put the receiver back on the hook. He took out a cigarette from his shirt pocket and lit it. He was tired after sleeping poorly through the night. He watched Martha open a large canister and sprinkle flour on the counter. "What are you doing?" he said.

Martha smiled. "Making tortillas," she said.

"We have thousands of tortillas in the freezer, and you're making tortillas." He exhaled a cloud of smoke. "Martha," he said, "my grandparents are driving around town in Ramona's truck. I don't know what to do."

For some reason, Martha thought that surely her grandfather-in-law must be too old to drive, and what would happen if he were stopped by the police? Without looking at her husband, she said, "What of his driver's license?"

Flavio stared at his wife and thought it was possible that everyone had gone crazy. He decided not to answer his wife's stupid question. He brought his cigarette to his mouth. "I'm going to get little José's things," he said, "and bring them to Ramona. And then we will see."

Ramona made sure José ate two bowls of cereal and then made him eat three pieces of toast that she coated thickly with butter and jam. She sat quietly across from him at the table and watched him eat. José ate as quickly as he could. He stared down at the table throughout the meal because he was afraid that if he inadvertently glanced at the platter of leftover food, Ramona would notice and force him to eat an enchilada.

When José had finished, Ramona told him to go ahead and dress in the clothes he had, but when Flavio arrived he would bathe and dress in clean clothes. José carried his bowl to the sink.

"Tía," he said, "where's my grandfather?"

"He's gone for a ride, José."

"Where?"

"I don't know," Ramona said. She didn't want to think about where her truck might be at this moment.

"He said we would irrigate again this morning."

"If he said that," Ramona said, "then he should be back soon. Do you know what to do?"

José shrugged. "You open the ditch so the water comes into the field."

"Yes, but it hasn't been done in a long time. You have to lead it slowly so that it sinks into the earth. Can you do that?"

"Yes," he said.

"You're not still hungry?"

"_____ osé said quickly and touched his stomach.

"_____ spoke for a moment, and then Ramona said _____ o then. When your grandfather comes, I'll _____ n you've already begun. And leave the mud _____ field, José."

Ramona straightened up the kitchen and swept the floor. When she was finished, she went to the door and pushed it open. Across the field, she could see José digging with the shovel. The alfalfa had grown greener from the rain the day before, but it was still stunted, and there were patches of bare dirt. She remembered that when she was young, her grandfather would sometimes cut this field three times in a summer. She watched José move quickly to his right, scraping the ground with his shovel.

Ramona poured herself another cup of coffee and sat at the table. She thought that if this were an ordinary day, she would get canvas from the shed and stretch it and gesso it, and by afternoon it would be dry and ready for oil. She thought that she would paint the sky as she had seen it the evening before, with such a myriad of colors that it dwarfed her grandfather and José. She had seen the sky as if it were alive, and she thought that if she could catch that feeling with her brush, her painting would move and breathe and not merely sit on the canvas and look back at her. If she were to let the brush go where it wished and not where she willed it. Then she looked down at the journal on the table. She brought her hand to her mouth and yawned and, as if it were of little matter, she reached out and moved the book closer.

FEBRUARY 5:
On this day, Lupita Valdez, the wife of Armando Valdez, gave birth to a baby girl who is to be named after her grandmother, Celestina Valdez.

FEBRUARY 6:
There was snow today in the mountains, but in the village there was only wind and cold. The clouds

cleared in the late afternoon, and this evening there
are stars.

FEBRUARY 9:
Elías Flores and his neighbor, Gilberto Tafoya, shot four
elk this morning before dawn. All four were cows and thin
from the winter. Elías and Gilberto shot them while the
herd, which numbered more than fifty, grazed on alfalfa
that Elías had placed not far from his home. The animals
were butchered, and the meat from two of them was divided
among those who helped, which were many.

The carcasses were left in the field, and after dark there
was the sound of coyotes.

FEBRUARY 11:
The road is now open to the south, as the weather has continued to be warm. Ramón Trujillo, who is my closest
neighbor, left this village without his family at dawn. He is
to seek work in the south, where planting has already begun.
His family is to follow if things go well for him.

When Ramona was sixteen years old, she walked
from her house to her grandparents'. She carried
baby José in her arms, and walking behind her and

kicking stones was Flavio. It had been in the summer when there was no wind, and the days were too hot without clouds, and even the grass was dry and brittle and coated with dust. Ramona's hair had been long then, far down her back, and she could feel the sweat on the back of her neck and against her chest where she carried José. As the three of them neared their grandparents', they passed by the Trujillo house that had been empty forever. Now there was a truck parked in the high weeds in front of it, and from inside the house they could hear hammering.

It was an old adobe, and a long time ago there had been a fire. Years after that, the north wall had washed away in heavy rains and the vigas had fallen, taking the roof with them. Ramona knew that the man who once lived there had left Guadalupe years and years ago, leaving his wife and children behind. Soon after, according to the story Ramona's grandmother had told her, the stovepipe had rusted through in the space above the ceiling, and the flames from the fire had licked at the latillas, and in the morning when the village woke, there was a cloud of black smoke hanging above this house. Inside, the wife and children of Ramón Trujillo lay dead in their beds, unburnt, their faces stained with soot. The house had sat empty ever since, and Ramón Trujillo had never returned to Guadalupe.

When Ramona and Flavio and José reached their grandparents' house that morning, their grandmother told Ramona that Juan Trujillo, Ramón's grandson from a later marriage, had come to Guadalupe. He had come from a place far to the south to claim the house his grandfather had built.

Sitting in her kitchen, so many years after that summer morning, Ramona was no longer looking at the book. Her eyes had gone somewhere else, and her hand moved slowly through her hair. She could no longer remember when she had actually met Juan Trujillo, but suddenly, in her life back then, he seemed to be everywhere around her. When she was at her grandparents', he would walk from his house with an empty jug for water. Sometimes he would stay for dinner. He would help her grandfather irrigate and go into the mountains and

haul firewood with her father. He would take
Flavio fishing along the creek, late in the day,
when he had finished working on his own house.
He was older than she, but not so much. His hair
was too long and his skin was dark, and when he
spoke to her there was a rhythm in his language
that Ramona had never heard before.

One night, late, when the house was still, she
drew Juan Trujillo. She drew the shape of his face
and traced the line of his neck and the curve of his
shoulder with her pencil. She drew until her body
became tense and her face flushed. Ramona didn't
sleep that night, and a few hours before dawn she
left her bed and walked across Guadalupe. There was
no moon, and the houses were dark. She wore only
her nightgown and nothing on her feet. By the time
she reached the house where Juan Trujillo lived, her
feet were scratched and her long hair was tangled
down her back. She remembered, even now, that she
stood outside his door and could feel the night air
on the backs of her legs and on her bare arms.

When Ramona left Guadalupe a few years later,
she left Juan Trujillo behind. One day, in one of

the few letters she received from her father, she read that the house Juan had rebuilt had caught fire again in the night. The following morning, he had spoken to no one but had packed what possessions remained and left Guadalupe.

Nothing remained now of the house Ramón Trujillo had once built. The adobe bricks had long ago washed to dirt. The vigas were gone, and weeds covered the few acres of land. Ramona thought there were many things in her life that she had almost forgotten. She rubbed at her eyes with her fingers and after a few moments looked back down at the journal.

FEBRUARY 12:

Father Joseph spoke with me today. He is a large man of German descent who speaks Spanish well but much too slowly. He has been priest here for thirty years and claims that his stay has been so long because the church has forgotten there is such a place as Guadalupe. He has told me privately in the past that he has received no correspondence from the archbishop in the last fifteen years and that, were it not for the parishes nearby, he would never know of changes

made in the church. I have asked him why he does not write
to his superiors to remind them not only of the existence of
this village but also of his presence in it, and he has said that
he fears they would then transfer him to a different parish,
and he would be lost.

Father Joseph told me he had visited the home of Berna
Ruiz a few days ago, as Berna's mother, who is ninety-six
years of age, was near death. Since then, she has miracu-
lously recovered and is now out of danger. Father Joseph
went on to say that Berna Ruiz's mother has become no
larger than a small child and can only breathe with her
mouth open wide. While he was there, Father Joseph noticed
that this woman was in possession of three santos I had
made, and while the two that were visible were carved with
great care and were pleasing to the eye and to the spirit, the
third stood in the far corner of the room, facing the wall,
with a small towel draped over its head.

When Father Joseph questioned Berna about this, she
told him, after much delay, that this particular santo was
responsible for the health of her family, and after her husband was injured last autumn when a tree he was felling
landed on his foot, and now with the illness of her mother,
she had placed the Lady in the far corner of the room with a

towel over her head so she could stare at nothing and see how she liked that. Father Joseph told her that he thought the Lady had learned her lesson and should be returned to the counter with her companions. Then he said it was quite possible that the Lady had been merely testing Berna's faith, as her husband had regained the strength in his foot and it now appeared that her mother would recover.

After telling me this, Father Joseph sat without speaking. I knew the three santos he spoke of. I had carved them a number of years ago. Two were small figures of Our Lady of Guadalupe, and the third was of Saint Francis that I had given Berna Ruiz as a gift when her son, Telesfor, married. All three were of cottonwood. I asked Father Joseph what he thought of this, and he responded that, although it was true God is everywhere, He is most present in the church. Father Joseph said he thought I should consider the santos I made to be the property of God and the church and that I should take care what homes I place them in. Surely a santo exiled to the corner of a room with a towel over her head was not something I wanted.

We spoke little more, and Father Joseph left before dark.

FEBRUARY 14:

*After mass today, I told Father Joseph that Our Lady of
Guadalupe would be completed before the following Sunday.
He seemed distracted and said that, although he has not seen
her, he trusts my talents. Upon leaving the church, Father
Joseph took me aside and asked what I thought of the saints
that were now being cast in plaster—that they were formed
in molds and in the time it took me to create one, thousands
could be made. I told Father Joseph that I thought not at all
about this and that, if I did, it would not be in a favorable
light.*

FEBRUARY 15:

*The weather remains warm and much of the snow has
melted. Andario Jaramillo came to my office on this day.
He told me that in the summer his daughter, Ofelia, will
marry the son of Romolo and Clorinda Gonzáles.*

FEBRUARY 16:

*Tonight I have finished Our Lady of Guadalupe. She
reaches to my chest, and I have given her the round face and
large eyes of my sister who died at the age of twelve. Her
gown is the color of blood and flows from her neck down to*

*the base she stands upon, which is the color of the earth. Her
hair is black and falls to her shoulders, and she stares for-
ward openly and without a smile. Her hands are raised
and meet at her chest, and I think it is in the thinness of the
fingers and the way they are bent slightly that I can see my
sister. She is to live in the church of this village to one side
of the altar, and upon the inside of her left wrist I have
traced with a knife the letters of my sister's name where
only I would find them. Ramona.*

Ramona stared at her name for a long time as if
she didn't recognize it written in another's hand.
She could hear the soft sound of her own breathing and nothing else. She felt as if the world had
somehow moved on and left her behind. She
thought that she should rouse herself, push the
book away from her, and let it fall to the floor
where the pages, brittle, would crack away from
the binding like ashes. Too many things were coming into her life, and she understood none of
them. Ramona closed her eyes and then, for the
first time, she wondered who this man was who
wrote such things, this man who had carved the

likeness of his sister, who bore her own name, onto a santo.

Ramona rose and walked to the kitchen door. Across the field, she could see José beating his shovel against the earth. She could see by the dark color of his pants that he was wet up to his crotch.

José had been losing his water to a gopher hole. By the size of this hole, José thought that a small dog could fall into it and become lost. His water, which he had so expertly led from the ditch, was pouring endlessly into the hole as if it fed to the other side of the world. José had tried to fill the hole with mud, but in so doing he had uncovered a maze of smaller holes and then had found himself suddenly surrounded by three small animals that ran around his legs making high-pitched barking noises. He was trying to smash one of them with the flat of his shovel when he heard his aunt's voice.

"José," Ramona called, "what are you doing?"

José pointed mutely at the ground.

"You are supposed to irrigate the field," Ramona yelled, "not beat it."

José nodded his head up and down, although he hadn't understood a word his aunt had said. He looked back at the ground and saw that the small animal he had been trying to smash had fled.

Ramona turned and went back into the kitchen, where she saw Flavio standing at the far end of the room. Against the wall were two large bags stuffed full.

"Ramona," Flavio said, "I've brought José's things. His clothes. Some books."

Ramona took in a deep breath. "Thank you, Flavio. I didn't hear your truck."

Flavio shrugged and then looked down at the floor. While rummaging through his brother's trailer, Flavio had planned a small speech to give to his sister. In this speech, he was to tell Ramona that she must be firm with their grandparents and tell them that this foolishness was something they would not allow. He had practiced this speech aloud a number of times until he thought he could recite it flawlessly. He had planned to tell Ramona these things immediately upon seeing her and then leave quickly for his house.

Flavio looked at his sister, and he saw the softness of her features and the redness in her eyes. He felt his plan slip away. "Are you all right, Ramona?" he said.

Ramona stared at her brother for a few seconds. "No," she said finally. "I'm not all right, Flavio. Nothing is what it should be. Whenever I turn around, there is something else." Ramona wondered why she was saying these things to her brother. She saw how awkward he looked, his hands stuffed in his pockets, his shoulders hunched up. "Maybe we should have a cup of coffee, Flavio," Ramona said, and then she smiled. "We can talk about how our grandparents are making us crazy."

Flavio sat across the table from his sister and sipped from the cup she had served him. "This is good coffee, Ramona," he said, although he thought the coffee tasted like mud.

"Grandmother made it," Ramona said.

"Ah," Flavio said. He remembered quite clearly the last time he and his sister had spoken about anything of meaning. It had been early in the morning the day after their mother's death, two days before Ramona disappeared from Guadalupe. Flavio had come into the kitchen to find Ramona at the sink. There had been a great many people in the house the day before, and the kitchen counters were piled high with pots and pans and platters of leftover food. Their father, in his sorrow, had consumed a bottle of whiskey, and Flavio and Ramona could hear the sound of his uneasy sleep through the wall.

"Flavio," Ramona had said, "when I'm gone, you must look after baby José."

Flavio, who had never cared to be near his younger brother because of the odd way the boy had of walking only backward, chose to ignore what his sister had said. "Ramona," he said, "do you think we will catch the same disease Mama had?"

Ramona's hands stopped moving, and she turned to her brother. Flavio thought she would be pretty if it weren't for the straightness of her mouth. "No," Ramona said. "Mama died of a sad heart. It is not something we will catch."

Flavio wondered how a sad heart could cause one's arms and legs to go numb. He heard his brother crying from another room.

"Where are you going, Ramona?" he asked.

"I'm going away," Ramona told him. "Forever."

Now, in another kitchen, Flavio placed the cup of coffee back on the table and folded his hands in his lap.

"Flavio," Ramona said, "it is not just our grandparents. Loretta is here too."

Flavio looked at Ramona blankly and then moved his eyes away. Out the open door, he saw how bright the sun was and then how a slight breeze moved the leaves of the cottonwoods. It will be a hot day, he thought. Maybe he would fish the creek later, where the trees shaded the water.

"Flavio," Ramona said, "are you listening?"

Flavio was suddenly overwhelmed with emotion, and a fear shot through him that he might weep and look like a fool before his sister. He cleared his throat and spoke carefully. "Yes," he said. "Loretta is here, también." My whole family, the living and the dead, Flavio thought, are roaming the streets of Guadalupe. "Why is this happening to us, Ramona?" he said.

It had not occurred to Ramona that her brother might feel as she did. She had always thought of Flavio as someone who was solid and dull and looked at life much the way a cow might. She stared at her brother and could see that the shape of his face, though heavier, was like hers and that he had shaved smoothly before leaving home. There was a streak of moisture at the corner of one eye, as if a wind were blowing in her kitchen. "I don't know, Flavio," she said.

"Maybe if you were to talk to our grandparents," Flavio said. "Tell them how disturbing this is."

Ramona sighed. "You think I haven't tried?" she said. "They are here as if they never left. Grandmother cooks and Grandfather irrigates. Loretta appears at odd times and is only concerned with little José."

"Is Loretta well?" Flavio asked.

"Is she well?" Ramona said.

"I mean . . . " Flavio began, and then for some peculiar reason he thought about how nice Loretta had always looked in blue jeans, but he chased away the thought before he mentioned it aloud. "I mean, Martha will be happy to hear this. She always enjoyed Loretta's company."

"That's good," Ramona said, and she suddenly had the distinct feeling that her conversation with her brother was going nowhere.

"Has Loretta spoken of our brother?"

"Barely," Ramona said, and she thought that possibly her dead brother had once again begun to do things backward.

"Ah," Flavio said. As a child, alone at night in his room, Flavio would sometimes practice death. He would lie stiffly in bed with his arms at his sides and quiet his breath. He would close his eyes lightly until he felt the muscles in his face relax and saw the colors beneath his eyelids turn to darkness. He would lie there so still and think that his legs were no longer attached to his body and, other than the occasional creak of a viga, he was encapsulated in a blackness that was, in its own way, comforting. This was what Flavio expected of death. Now it was beginning to appear that death more closely resembled the annual church picnic where everyone ate lamb with their fingers, drank a little too much beer, and threw horseshoes.

"Maybe if we talk to the priest," Flavio said. "He could intervene on our behalf."

Ramona pictured Father Leonardo and her grandfather in the same room together. "I don't think that is a good idea, Flavio," she said.

Actually, Flavio didn't either. His grandfather spoke only in monosyllables, and about him was always an air of impatience. Father Leonardo led mass in much the way that one would lead a marching band. His grandfather and the priest in the same room would be a disaster.

"I thought," Ramona said, "that you as the oldest grandson should talk with our grandfather."

"Me?" Flavio said. He stared at his sister. He saw that she was smiling slightly, and he wondered if she were teasing him.

"Yes," Ramona answered, and she realized she was taking pleasure in her brother's discomfort. "I have had to live and sleep with them. It is the least you can do."

"Grandfather has disliked me since the day I killed his chicken," Flavio said. "It is you who were always his favorite, Ramona."

"It was the lie you told to him."

"It was an accident. How was I to know the chicken would be in a tree?"

Ramona grunted. "No one has ever believed that story, Flavio."

"It's the truth," he said. "I swear."

"Roosters do not make nests in trees, Flavio."

"Possibly not all roosters," Flavio said. Then he and Ramona heard Ramona's truck pulling into the driveway.

SIX

RAMONA WATCHED HER GRANDMOTHER rush into the kitchen. She was dressed in the same clothes she had been wearing the day before, and her dress was rumpled from sitting in the truck. There was a faint line of lipstick on her grandmother's lips.

"Flavio," Rosa said breathlessly. "Oh, how good it is to see you, hijo." She walked quickly up behind her grandson and put her hands on his shoulders. She bent over and placed her cheek against Flavio's ear. "It's been so long, hijo," she said softly. "So very long I've missed my grandson." Ramona watched her brother close his eyes. One of her grandmother's hands patted Flavio's shoulder. "Tonight we eat your favorite food," Rosa said. "Enchiladas with cilantro. The way you like them."

Ramona saw Flavio's face knot up, and to her amazement, her brother began to cry.

Flavio felt as though he had left his body and was watching from above. He saw his grandmother as he had always remembered her, with her cheek pressed against the side of his face and her hand patting his shoulder. He saw how his head had fallen to his chest, that he was gulping air soundlessly, and that there were tears streaming like a river down his face. He also saw that his sister was staring at him with an expression of astonishment.

Ramona was thinking that her brother cried exactly as he had as a child, and she remembered the times she had joyfully tormented him until his face would twist as it did now and he would run from her.

Ramona heard her grandfather's voice. "Look at you," Epolito said gruffly. "Bawling like a baby. What's wrong with you?"

Flavio wiped at his face with the flat of his hand. He opened his mouth as if to speak and then closed it. Ramona glanced back at her grandfather, who was standing just inside the kitchen door. "Grandfather," she said.

"What have you done to your brother?" he said.

"Nothing. We were just talking."

"And this is what happens when you talk to your brother?"

"My hijo is just a little upset," Rosa said, still patting Flavio's shoulder.

"Enough of this," Epolito said. "Stop this nonsense, Flavio. Your nephew is out in the field irrigating, and you sit in here with the women crying like a small dog. What's wrong with you, anyway?" Epolito turned and looked out across the field at José, who was no longer irrigating but had built a wall of mud and was busy running back and forth where the water ate through. "Flavio," Epolito said.

Flavio shook his head. "Yes, Grandfather," he said. "I have a shovel in my truck. I'll get it and come to the field."

Ramona watched her brother rise without looking at her. He walked out of the room, and Ramona heard the sound of the front door opening and closing.

Rosa pulled out the chair in which Flavio had been sitting. "This has been a long day, and still it's morning," she said. "And oh yes, Ramona, before I forget, your grandfather says there is a noise in your truck and that you should fix it before the engine blows up."

"I drive the truck seldom, Grandmother," Ramona said. "And then only around town."

"Things blow up even around town, Ramona. You could turn the key and be in flames. We wouldn't want that, hija."

Ramona closed her eyes for a moment. When she opened them, she said, "I will have the truck looked at."

"Good," Rosa said. "Maybe Flavio would do this."

"Yes," Ramona said. Her brother passed by the kitchen window. He was walking quickly, his hat pulled down low on his forehead. As soon as he disappeared from sight at the window, he reappeared at the kitchen door.

"Ramona," he said.

"Hijo," Rosa said, "you look so good. Did I tell you?"

Flavio smiled. "Yes, Grandmother." He looked at his sister. "Ramona, will you call Martha?"

"And tell her what?"

"Tell her we will be eating here and to stop making tortillas." Flavio looked back at his grandmother. "If that is all right."

"How can you ask such a thing?" Rosa said. "And I will call Martha. It's been too long since I talked with her."

Flavio hesitated for a second, and then he said, "Thank you, Grandmother. Well . . . " and after standing there for a moment, he turned and walked away.

"He's a good boy," Rosa said, smiling.

"Yes," Ramona said, but what she thought was that her life was being completely disrupted by her grandmother. She also thought that there were not enough chairs in her house to seat Flavio and Martha and José, her grandparents, and herself.

"Alfonso Vigil and his son will be coming for dinner, también," Rosa said.

"You are having a party here, Grandmother?" Ramona asked.

"A little party, hija. We spent this morning with Alfonso. It will be good for him to get out of his house."

Ramona remembered Alfonso Vigil as a large man who, when drinking, would often dance by himself in small circles and smile down at his feet. He had been a close friend of her grandfather's and would sometimes walk to their home on summer evenings with his own grandchildren.

"I didn't think Alfonso was still alive," Ramona said.

"That's because all you do, Ramona, is sit here by yourself." Rosa leaned over the table and lowered her voice nearly to a whisper. "He is so old, hija. One hundred and four. You remember his face, which was always so full and round? Well, now it is nothing but ears and bone. Not even his hair grows anymore. There is something like dust on the top of his head. And I swear to you, he is smaller even than I."

Ramona looked down at her grandmother's hands, which were folded together on top of the table. She saw how the knuckles were swollen and slightly discolored, how some of the fingers did not bend with the others. "Alfonso Vigil is coming here for dinner," Ramona said, more to herself than to her grandmother.

"Yes," Rosa said. "With his son, Albert, who will drive him."

Ramona looked back up at her grandmother. "You saw his son?"

"Only in leaving and then from the truck. I don't think he recognized us."

"And Alfonso," Ramona said, "was he surprised to see you?"

Rosa leaned a little closer to her granddaughter. "When the poor man breathes, you cannot see his chest move. It is like he is the walking dead." Here Rosa crossed herself.

Ramona stared at her grandmother. "Grandmother," she said, "you and Grandfather are dead."

Rosa sat up straight in her chair. "You think," she said, "that I don't know that?"

"But if you know, then you must realize that this is not where you belong."

"I don't belong here? In my own house? How can you say such a thing, Ramona?"

Ramona tried to keep her voice calm. "Grandmother, why are you here? Why is Grandfather out irrigating with Flavio and José? Why does Loretta suddenly appear as if from nowhere?"

"Loretta?" Rosa said, looking to each side of her. "I haven't seen Loretta. When have you seen Loretta?"

Ramona thought that she should run from the kitchen. She thought it unfair that someone like herself, who seldom spoke to anyone, should have a conversation such as this.

"Grandmother," she said, "please."

Rosa placed her hand on her chest. "You think I can answer these things?"

"If you can't," Ramona said, "who can?"

"How do I know that, Ramona?" Rosa said, and she dropped her hand to her lap. "Why are we

having such a stupid talk? There are people coming here today, and I sit wasting time. There's
Martha to call. Flavio married well. There are no
children, but one cannot ask for everything. But
you, Ramona, alone here."

At this moment, Ramona felt as if she had never
been alone. For the past twelve years, she had spent
almost all her time in solitude. She would walk the
hills behind her house, often walking beyond them
into the valley where the river had gouged out the
earth. There, Ramona would sit for hours and
watch the water flow hundreds of feet below her.
Sometimes she would drive her grandfather's truck
into the mountains on old roads and return home
late with the truck bed piled high with branches of
piñon and juniper that she burned in her stove in
the winter. There were days when Ramona would
paint from early in the morning until after dark, as
though there were no such thing as time. And now
her life had suddenly become crowded. As soon as
one person walked out of her house, another
walked in. And, she thought, no one even knows

to knock. She shook her head a little and then said, "I'll help you cook, Grandmother."

"No," Rosa said, "Martha can help with that. You take your book."

Ramona looked down at the journal, which sat on the table between them. "Who is the man who wrote these things, Grandmother?" she said.

Rosa got up from her chair with a small grunt and went to the counter. She got an apron from one of the drawers and tied it high around her waist. "He was your grandfather's first cousin," she said. "He lived not far from here in the house his father built. It was just a little past our field at the foot of the hill. It was torn down with tractors many years ago when the mine bought all that land. I think there are some posts, but the house is gone." Rosa crossed her arms and looked at her granddaughter. "His sister died as a young girl, and soon after his mother went crazy and left this village. It was a sad thing, Ramona. She left her son alone with his father, who knew nothing about the welfare of a child. It is easy to forget that even people from here can go crazy." To Ramona, this was the most sane statement her grandmother had made.

Rosa leaned toward her granddaughter and, in a whisper, said, "No one knows whatever became of her, hija. She packed her belongings in a carton and came down to the road and stood there by herself, as if waiting for something. And this was many years before there were such things as buses, Ramona. I remember this quite clearly. For three days and three nights this woman stood there waiting for no one knew what and listening to no one. Her husband begged her to return and at night would cover her shoulders with a blanket. We would see her in the morning standing there like an Indian. And then, on the morning of the fourth day, she was gone. On the ground was the small carton full of her things and the blanket." Rosa leaned back against the counter. "So you see," she said.

Two things occurred to Ramona. The first was that things seemed to be expanding around her until everything her grandmother had said was so vast that there was nothing her senses could rest upon. The second was that the response her grandmother had given her didn't have a thing to do with the question she had asked. She picked up the book from the table. "Grandmother," she said.

Rosa looked at her granddaughter for a moment and then said, "His name was Antonio Montoya. He was named after his own grandfather and was of our family. For a little while he kept the records of this village. And, like you, he never married and was careless with himself." Rosa pushed away from the counter. "Now go, Ramona. There are things to do."

Ramona walked to the kitchen door. In the field, she could see her grandfather and Flavio working side by side. Little José was behind them, throwing clumps of mud. She thought that by now he must be filthy.

"He's fine," Rosa said. "He's with his grandfather."

"Yes," Ramona said.

"He's a good boy, isn't he, hija?"

"Yes," Ramona said again. "I think he is." She stepped outside and walked around to the front yard. Loretta was walking up to the house.

"Good morning, Ramona," she said and smiled. Loretta was dressed in blue jeans and a light red blouse that was ruffled at the ends of the short sleeves. Ramona could smell the odor of mint on her breath.

"Good morning, Loretta," Ramona said.

"It's a beautiful day, isn't it?"

"Yes," Ramona said, "it is."

"Grandmother is in the house?"

"Yes. In the kitchen. She's cooking."

"I'll surprise her. You look so nice this morning, Ramona." Loretta walked by her into the house.

Ramona sat down in the wicker chair beneath the cottonwood. From inside the house, she heard Loretta speak her grandmother's name and then the sound of Rosa's voice saying loudly, "Loretta, is that you? Ramona said you were here. I'm so glad. Let me look at you."

Octaviana Esquibel was an old woman when Ramona was a young girl, and before dawn each day, Octaviana would walk the long distance to the church. She always wore a black shawl that wrapped around her head and face and covered her shoulders, and for a woman whose body was bent with age, Octaviana walked with quick, sure steps. In the empty church, she would sit at the back and argue loudly with herself. If the church door was open, her voice would carry in the morning air like the crow of a rooster. One Sunday, Ramona had been late for mass, and she had sat beside Octaviana, who was always loudest when people were around. Ramona had gone through this mass with her eyes closed, praying that Octaviana would not be disruptive and embarrass her. Near the end of the service, Octaviana had suddenly leaned close to Ramona and, with her breath on Ramona's face, had said loudly, "Do you see them, hija? Above the priest's head are forty-seven babies, and none of them are happy." Then she had leaned back. "Eee," she had said, "that one on the end looks like trouble." Ramona had spent the remainder of the mass staring at the air above the priest's head. As Ramona sat beneath the cottonwood listening to her grandmother and Loretta visit in her kitchen, she thought that Octaviana would have enjoyed being at her house, that she would not have been out of place in the present company.

Ramona stretched out her legs and looked across the road at the old village office. It looked no different to her than it ever had, a neglected building of mud and boards that was of no use to anyone. Someday soon, it would collapse in on itself. Ramona thought that if she closed her eyes, she would see the structure without the sag in the roof and with the walls newly mudded. She would see snow drifted against the walls, trails of footsteps, and the dim glow of a kerosene lamp. Past the building, she could see much of the village of Guadalupe. She could see how the village was settled in a small valley at the base of the Sangre de Cristo mountains, how the creek, lined with full growth, meandered through the center of the valley, and how the maze of smaller ditches, like arteries, branched off from it through fields of alfalfa. She could see the roof of Flavio's house, where she was born, where her parents had lived. From far behind her in the field, she heard the sound of her brother's voice. The sun was shining through the branches of the cottonwood, and she could feel its heat upon her face.

FEBRUARY 17:
The wind blows bitterly from the north, and it is too cold for this month. This morning, Melquiades Cortéz shot the windows out of his house from the inside. He told me he shot in such a way as not to harm his children. He was not drunk, and when I asked him why he would do such a thing, he did not answer. He is a tall, thin man who looks only at the ground when he walks and speaks seldom to anyone. As he has four young children, and his wife died bearing the last, I feel that I will speak to his brother, Tomás, about their care. I and Melquiades's oldest son, Andrés, boarded up the windows and covered them with cloth to keep out the wind. I have taken his rifle and will give it to his brother.

FEBRUARY 18:
On the evening of this day, Father Joseph came to my house. He walked with a lantern, as there is no moon, and upon

arriving spent much time complaining of the wind and how this winter seemed an eternity. We spoke of the trouble at the home of Melquiades Cortéz, and he agreed it would be wise to talk to Tomás now rather than after a tragedy. We spoke little after that, and as it was becoming late, I asked if he wished to see Our Lady. He sat without speaking for some time and then rose from his chair and stood by the stove. He said he had walked to my house at such a late hour with a purpose, and now that he was here it was a difficult thing to speak of. I reminded him that he had been priest in this village for thirty years, that he had baptized and wed and buried so many from here that there should be little the two of us could not discuss. He agreed that our relationship has always been one of respect and that we had always worked together for the well-being of the people of Guadalupe. He said that there was no reason for this situation to change, but he had given much thought to the nature of my work with santos and, although he held my craftsmanship in the highest esteem, he felt that the keeping of santos had begun to resemble idolatry and that it would be best for all if I ceased to create such things.

He said that he knew from talks with other priests that other parishes had put a stop to this behavior many years

*ago and that it was time for Guadalupe to follow their
example. He said that in the summer he would order from
a city in the east a number of plaster saints to replace those
I had made. I did not respond, and he said that it would be
best if the Lady I had completed were to remain with me,
and also that it would ease his mind if I would no longer
present these things to the people of this village. He said that
at mass the following day he would speak of these matters to
all. We spoke no more after this.*

FEBRUARY 19:
*The wind has left but has brought clouds that do not move
and sit low on the mountains.*

FEBRUARY 20:
*On this day my mother was born. She was christened
Carmela Ramírez, and she would be fifty-seven years
of age.*

Ramona's mother died in her sleep. Her father
had awakened beside his wife and spoken her
name, and she lay there with her eyes half open
and a soft smile on her mouth as if she had gone
to a place she wished to be. She had always been a

woman whom life could wear down. Even when Ramona was young, when her mother would laugh or sometimes dance or there was sweat on her face from some excitement, Ramona knew in her heart that her mother would never be old. She was often ill and would take to bed for long periods of time, and the activities in the house would continue about her, although hushed, as if a spirit lived amongst them. Although it was true that her mother was not strong, Ramona was aware that she preferred to spend much of her life away from others. During these times, Ramona would bring her meals and would sit beside her mother on the bed. Across the room was a large window, and out it you could see the mountains and all of the sky. Her mother would eat slowly, and she would talk.

"See there, mi hija. That deep canyon where the aspens are like cloth and there are rocks with the faces of lions. There is a spring in that place that empties into a pool that is dark with shadows from the trees. You can walk a trail only animals use and sit beside this pool of water, and the trees around it will tell you things. They will tell stories of young girls who were so brave, and foolish too, that they left this place and wandered into the mountains and became lost. In places, the creeks would run uphill and in circles and up waterfalls, and it was impossible for these young girls to find their way out. They would walk and walk until they finally came to this pool of water, and they would sit beside it, and through the branches of the aspens they could see this valley and how far they had come. If they drank from this water, and they always did, mi hija, they would sleep forever and only dream of quiet things. In the winter, this pool would never freeze, but green things would grow beside it and there would be steam. And nothing there would ever be forgotten. . . . "

Ramona would lie close beside her mother and look out the window at the mountains, and she would see herself walking the paths only animals used. Sometimes she would fall asleep to the sound of her mother's voice.

Ramona's eyes were still on the journal, though she was no longer reading. She moved her hand slowly and turned the page.

FEBRUARY 21:

There is six inches of new snow, and already I believe there to be more snow than all of last season. In the spring, the ditches will run full.

FEBRUARY 22:

This morning, upon arriving at the village office, I found a santo that had been left standing outside the door. Two inches of fresh snow lay upon her head and her shoulders, and laid beneath her feet was a small piece of cloth. I had made her two summers ago and given her to Andamo Santistevan, as he and his wife, Estelle, were greatly concerned about their infant daughter, Alicia, who was four months old and who would no longer take nourishment. Soon afterward, Andamo had returned to my house to tell me that he and his wife had placed the santo beside the bed of their daughter, and within days she began to take milk from her mother and in a week gained three pounds. I remember the santo well, as I cut myself deeply in carving the bend of her right elbow and could not entirely remove the stain of blood from the wood. She stands to just above my knee and smiles slightly, with her head bowed. Other than a small chip on her chin, she appears to have been well cared for.

FEBRUARY 23:

On this day I spoke with Tomás Cortéz about the care of his brother's children. He told me that although there is little room in his house, he has already spoken with his wife, and they plan to bring the children to live with them. He agreed that this is for the best. I have begun work on a new Lady, which goes poorly. In my house now is the santo once belonging to Andamo and Estelle Santistevan and the santo which bears the likeness of my sister. Both stand side by side.

FEBRUARY 24:

Epolito Montoya came to the office as I was leaving and walked with me to my home. I had not seen his son, Lito, for some days, and when I mentioned this, he told me that Lito had climbed the ladder that rests against the side of their house and crawled through the small trapdoor that leads into the attic space, in which there is nothing but cobwebs and the dirt that covers the wood ceiling. From there, he had jumped

into a snowbank in which was buried a large pile of stones
that Epolito had gathered last autumn. Lito had not broken
any bones in this leap but had hit his head and now asks the
same question over and over again and has been unsteady
on his feet for four days. Upon arriving at my house,
Epolito told me that his wife, Rosa, has recently been
troubled and that he wished for me to speak with her. I
told him that I would do this and that the following day
I would come to his house.

FEBRUARY 25:

In the afternoon, I walked to the house of my cousin, which
sits no more than one hundred yards to the west of the village office. Rosa Montoya greeted me at the door. She is a
strong, small woman with braided hair that falls far down
her back. She is a woman who speaks what is in her mind
and has been this way since a child. We sat in the kitchen,
which is a dark room this time of the year with only one
small window above the sink. I asked Rosa about the health
of her son. She told me he was no better, and then she began
to weep. She wept without making a sound and did not bow
her head. I told her I was certain her son would recover,
that head injuries often linger for many days and that if it

continued, with the roads open it would be of little difficulty to transport him to Las Sombras.

Rosa apologized for acting foolishly and said that Lito was only one part of her problem. I told her that I would do whatever I could, and she then told me that for fourteen nights she had been dreaming the same dream, and in this dream she sees the cemetery of Guadalupe on fire. . . .

SEVEN

MARTHA HAD JUST FINISHED warming the last of forty-eight tortillas on her stove when the phone in her kitchen rang. The ring was especially shrill in the closed-in heat of the room, and Martha found herself hurrying to the phone as if it were important that it not make the same sound twice.

"Hija," the voice said when Martha answered, and suddenly she felt as if she should be sitting down. She leaned back against the wall and felt the dampness of her blouse against her skin.

"Grandmother Rosa?" she said in a voice like a child's.

"You remember, hija," Rosa said. "And after such a long time."

"Yes," Martha said softly, and she stared down at her bare feet, which were dusted with flour from the tortillas. She moved her toes up and down.

"I'm so proud of you I can't tell," Rosa said. "Flavio looks so good. And so happy. You have done well with him. I'm so proud, Martha."

Martha remembered her wedding day, when grandmother Rosa had approached her quietly and in all seriousness. She had held Martha's hand tightly and told her that she was a Montoya now and also which foods Flavio was especially fond of.

"You must come here, hija," Rosa said. "The weather is too hot to be alone with yourself."

"I should come there?" Martha said, and again she could hear the sound of a small girl in her voice.

"Yes. Come and help us cook."

"Is Flavio there?"

"He's in the field with his grandfather and little José," Rosa said, and then she lowered her voice. "And there is a surprise for you. Loretta is here."

"Loretta?" Martha said and found she was smiling.

José Sr. had gotten Loretta pregnant one night in late winter in the front seat of his brother's truck.

Earlier that same evening, Loretta had been walking on the shoulder of the road with her friend Giselle when José slowed his brother's pickup alongside them and rolled down the passenger window. Loretta was dressed in her father's coat, and although she was warm, it hung on her body and made her look like a child. Giselle had her coat slung back off both shoulders. She was wearing a pink sweater that showed the size of her breasts. She had sneakers on her feet, her ankles bare to the cold. Giselle was freezing, and when José pulled up alongside them, Giselle wondered if he had the heater on and if Loretta would be truly angry at her when she left with José. José took the truck out of gear and let it roll at the speed Loretta and Giselle were walking.

"Hey," he said and gave Giselle a smile. He had shaved just an hour earlier, and the skin on his face felt smooth and tight. "Giselle," he said, "I'll give you a ride."

Giselle, without a glance at him but with a smile, said, "Where, José?"

"Anywhere," José said. It was then that Loretta walked around her friend and without a word climbed into the truck. José looked at Loretta as if something had flown into the cab of his brother's pickup. José thought that he would take this girl home quickly and then race back for Giselle.

On the drive to Loretta's house, Loretta slipped off her father's coat and shook her hair free. She sank back into the seat. "José," she said, without looking at him, "when we were in school, it was you I always watched."

They parked out at the gorge above the river, in the midst of crusted snow and sagebrush and a black sky filled with too many stars. They drank a little whiskey that José had hidden under the seat, and Loretta sat close to her door and watched how José's breath fogged the windows.

Years later, Loretta would tell her sister-in-law, Martha Montoya, that she didn't know what had possessed her that night. In what seemed like a long time but was actually a long moment, Loretta's white panties were on the floor of the pickup, and her slacks along with her blouse and bra were lying where José had been sitting. She marveled at the speed of José's hands and at the overwhelming sensation within her as if she were sucking this boy's whole being into the small area between her legs. In a second, Loretta thought she had found the way to spend the rest of her life.

When they were finished, Loretta was lying flat on the seat with her head on the armrest. She looked at José, who was still clothed except for his open zipper. She thought he looked embarrassed. She thought he looked foolish still in his clothes.

"José," she said, "I want to do this again," and twenty minutes later little José sprang to life in her womb.

Driving to Ramona's house, Martha thought of this story that Loretta had told her long ago. She remembered the sound of Loretta's voice and how it would rise in tone when she laughed and how she would speak as if out of breath.

Martha turned her small car off the highway near the village office. Beside her on the front seat were the forty-eight tortillas, three dozen pork tamales, and a large box of biscochitos. The interior of Martha's car was stifling from sitting in the sun, and it smelled like her kitchen.

As Martha pulled in carefully between Ramona's and Flavio's vehicles, she saw Ramona sitting beneath the large cottonwood in the front yard. Ramona's eyes were closed, and her head was bent back slightly as if she were sunning herself. Beyond Ramona, Martha could see the front of the house. She didn't know what she had expected, but it looked as old and empty as it ever had. It occurred to her that what she was doing was crazy, and she was thinking that she should quietly back up her car and drive home when she saw Ramona's eyes open. Martha climbed out of the car and closed the door gently.

"Good morning, Martha," Ramona said.

Martha took a few steps toward her sister-in-law and then stopped. She could feel the heat from the sun lying heavily upon her. "I'm sorry to disturb you, Ramona," she said.

Ramona smiled. "You're not disturbing me, Martha. I'm glad you came."

Martha looked at the book lying closed on Ramona's lap and thought it was something that had been under the earth for a long time. Even from where she was standing, she could smell the odor of dirt. "Grandmother Rosa called me," she said.

"Yes," Ramona said. "I think she is calling everyone."

"Then it's true."

"Oh, sí. It's true. It's so true that I think maybe it is us who have been wrong all this time."

"And Loretta?"

"También."

For a moment Martha said nothing. Finally she waved her arm behind her. "I have tortillas in the car. And tamales."

Ramona nodded, and at that moment the front door of the house swung open. "Martha," Loretta sang out. Martha's eyes widened. Her mouth fell open, and her face twisted.

Loretta ran past Ramona and embraced Martha. When they separated, Ramona could see that Martha's face was wet and shining.

"I thought . . . " Martha said.

"I know," Loretta said.

"But . . . "

"It doesn't matter, Martha. It's like waking in the morning after a dream."

"But Loretta . . . " Suddenly Martha's eyes met Ramona's. They looked at each other for no more than a few seconds, and in that glimpse both saw nothing but the other. Then Loretta took Martha's hands and pulled her arms gently.

"Come," she said. "We're making a feast."

Martha looked at Loretta. "Flavio is here?"

"Yes, Martha, he's in the field with José and Grandfather. Come."

Martha glanced behind her at her car. "I've brought tortillas," she said.

The two women walked together to the car and unloaded the food Martha had brought. They walked past Ramona, their arms full, and when they reached the house, Ramona heard the creaking

of the hinges and then the sound of her grandmother's voice. "Mi hija," she said.

*. . . We did not speak for some time. In the next room, I
could hear Lito stir in his sleep. He spoke aloud and said,
"Mama, am I still here?" Rosa answered with only her
breath, and she said, "Yes, mi hijo, you are still here with
us." And then Lito too fell silent. Rosa stared at me, and
although her eyes were still damp, she smiled.*

*She said that she did not mean to trouble me with her
problems, but Epolito had been concerned for some days, and
as our families had been close, she had agreed to speak with
me. I told her I would do all I could but that I knew little
of such things. I did know that for more than thirty days
this winter, fires had burned in the cemetery in order to dig
graves and that it was possible it was from this that her
dreams came. Rosa nodded but did not stop smiling and told
me, as if I were a child, that no one dreams the same dream
for fourteen nights.*

*She said that in this dream the fires were different, as
though the cemetery were burning inside the earth, and the
flames grew from each grave like blossoms, and the smoke
lay black and thick above the ground.*

I did not know what to say other than that I thought
the dream would pass in time, and if she were further disturbed, she should speak with Father Joseph. At this, Rosa
stopped smiling and sat back in her chair and crossed her
arms. She told me that she had attended mass last Sunday
and noticed that I had not. She had heard the priest say
that the keeping of santos in their homes was idolatry and
something neither God nor the church would allow any
longer.

I told Rosa it seemed as though we had strayed from
the subject of her dreams and that if there were differences
between Father Joseph and myself, this did not mean he
could not be of assistance to her. At this, Rosa reached
across the table and touched my hand. She asked me if I
knew what she was requesting, and after a moment, I told
her that I did and that in the morning before light I would
return to her house.

Outside my door when I returned home was a santo
I had never seen before. It is a small figure of Our Lady of
Guadalupe and so old that the paint on her face has peeled
and there is a split in the wood that runs from the top of
her neck through her torso. In the darkness outside my house,
I stumbled over her and broke a finger on her left hand.

FEBRUARY 26:

This morning before dawn I walked to my cousin's house. The air was warm, and in it was the scent of a new season. The windows were dark, but as I approached, the door opened and I was met by Rosa. She nodded and did not speak, and I entered and stood the santo I had carried, which bears the likeness of my sister, before her. I asked her if in the night she had dreamed, and without looking at me she said yes, softly, and she took my hand and brought it to her lips.

FEBRUARY 27:

This morning, Benito Medina came to my office. He and his family live two miles north of this village, where the land becomes flat and treeless and remains so for a hundred miles beyond. His nose and eyes were wet from the wind, and in his beard below his mouth were small pieces of ice. He had walked this distance to town to inform me that he had been cheated by his cousin, Horacio Medina. He told me that a week ago he had bought a horse from Horacio for forty dollars and that he planned to use this horse in taking his sheep to pasture in the spring. Horacio had assured Benito of the good health of this animal, and it wasn't until

Benito returned home that he discovered the horse to be blind in both eyes. When he returned to Horacio's home to complain, Horacio had refused to reimburse him, stating that an agreement had been made and that it was no matter if the horse was blind, as there was nothing of importance for it to see where Benito lived. I told Benito I would speak with Horacio in the afternoon.

Late in the day, I walked to the home of Horacio Medina, and we spoke outside his house. He is a strong, stocky man with teeth that are too large for his mouth and the father of six daughters who all resemble him and who are not seen outside their house other than at mass each Sunday. I told Horacio that Benito had asked me to intervene in the recent sale of a horse. At this, Horacio turned away and, looking at the mountains, told me that this was a business that had nothing to do with me, and he did not choose to waste his time discussing it.

I have stopped my work on the new Lady, as I can see nothing in the wood.

Ramona stopped reading, and the words "I can see nothing in the wood" washed over and through her in a wave of grief that was almost a caress.

Behind her, from inside the house, she could hear the soft murmur of voices, and on the street before her she could see heat rising from the pavement. She felt tired and thought that it would be nice to lean back in her chair and close her eyes. She also thought that with her eyes closed she would see her next painting, and in this painting would be the cemetery of Guadalupe. She would paint flowers and pure white crosses and the sun in the weeds, and in the cemetery would be a thin white flame. At this thought, Ramona actually closed her eyes, and she watched the flames spread and burn the high grass and the weeds along the fence until the fire had cleansed the ground, until only the crosses and the flowers remained, as if they would be there forever. In her mind she could see this painting move and breathe on the canvas. She thought that she might do a number of these paintings and that together they would be the story of a place and that each one would be painted on a large canvas and that she would only allow these paintings to leave the village of Guadalupe after they had been viewed here.

Although, Ramona thought, not at her home, as there were already too many people wandering about.

Behind her, the door to the house opened and closed softly. Ramona heard the sound of footsteps and then Loretta's voice.

"Are you sleeping, Ramona?"

"No, Loretta," Ramona said. "I was dreaming." Loretta was kneeling beside her chair. Her skin was smooth and flushed from being in the kitchen, and there was a brush of chile powder on her cheek.

"I've brought you coffee, Ramona, and some biscochitos."

Ramona pushed herself up straight in the chair and took the cup and small plate from Loretta. "I've done nothing but eat the last two days," she said. "Thank you."

"It's nothing," Loretta said as she leaned back to sit on the grass. She wrapped her arms around her knees. "Eee, it's hot. Even in the shade. I don't remember this much heat in August. I think in the kitchen it must be one hundred degrees."

Ramona ate a biscochito, which was still cold from Martha's freezer. "I'll come and help," she said. "I've sat out here long enough."

"There is nothing to do. You are better out here. Grandmother Rosa and Martha are working like little machines, and all I do is keep the pans clean. If you were to come in, you would just sweat in the heat and make the room warmer."

Ramona's neighbor to the south, Fabian Martínez, drove slowly past the house in his truck, which had two flat tires. Ramona could see how tightly he was gripping the steering wheel and how he jerked his chin up and down in greeting without looking away from the road.

"Loretta," Ramona said, "I think we should talk about José."

"My son."

"Yes," Ramona said. "Your son."

"You want to tell me that he shouldn't live here with you."

"No," she said. "I want to tell you that I don't know how to raise a child. I think that this may not be for the best."

Loretta leaned toward her sister-in-law and placed her hand on Ramona's arm. "From inside the kitchen I can see him in the field with his grandfather and his Tío Flavio, and I can see how happy he is here."

Ramona turned and looked at Loretta. "It has only been one day, Loretta."

"One day, one year," Loretta said and shrugged her shoulders. "You think there is something to know about raising a child? You feed them. You yell at them when they do wrong, and you make sure they take a bath."

"You make it sound like having a dog."

"You think there is a big difference? With girls, maybe. But boys . . . "

"This is not what I meant, Loretta," Ramona said.

"I know what you meant," Loretta said. "I would not have asked you to do this if it was wrong. I am his mother, Ramona, and if I cannot be with him, I wish for him to be here. With you."

From behind the house, Ramona heard Flavio's voice and then the sound of José's feet running.

She looked back at Loretta. "Your son is coming," she said.

Loretta turned her head away. "See how the heat rises from the road," she said. "You can see the air. Ramona, I know it shouldn't be, but I wish to hold my son again."

From the corner of her eye, Ramona saw José round the corner of the house. "Tía," he said, and then he fell quiet.

Loretta turned toward him and held out her arms. José ran to her and fell into his mother's arms as if he were a part of her body. Ramona looked down at her coffee and saw in it the shadow of her face.

"Why did you trick me?" José said, his voice muffled by Loretta's blouse.

Loretta held him tighter, and her voice made a soft humming sound. "There has been no trick, mi hijo," she said.

José raised his head. "So we're going home?"

Loretta kissed his mouth. "No, José," she said, and then she kissed his eyes. "It was a very bad accident. I came back because I love you so very much. And also to see if your Tía Ramona has made sure you bathed, which I can see she hasn't." Loretta placed her hand on José's cheek. "I can only stay a little while, hijo."

"Until I'm older."

"Until it's time to go."

"And then you'll be gone?"

"Yes," Loretta said. "Like smoke that is magic. And you are to stay with your Tía Ramona, where I can always see you. You are to listen to her always. Always, José."

José turned his eyes to Ramona. He didn't speak, and they looked at each other while Loretta's hand softly stroked the side of José's face. Ramona felt as though the three of them had fallen into a painting.

"Come," Loretta said. "Let's see what Grandmother Rosa has made."

MARCH 1:
For the past two days the wind has taken much of the moisture from the snow, which has shrunk to no more than six inches on the ground. There is mud now in the

afternoons. Lito Montoya, the son of Epolito and Rosa Montoya, returned to school this morning for the first time since his accident. He walked alone, and I watched him make his way carefully across the crust of snow. On his forehead was a white bandage.

MARCH 2:

Today Isaac Medina, the oldest son of Benito Medina, shot the blind horse his father had purchased, and also Horacio Medina. The shootings occurred outside the home of Horacio Medina, and when I arrived, Isaac was sitting alone in the road near the body of the large horse. From inside the house came the noise of many women and the loud voice of Horacio. Isaac told me that he had come to Horacio's house early in the morning to return the horse his father had been cheated into buying, and upon hearing this Horacio had called his father a name he would not repeat. At this, Isaac said, he had shot his rifle at the ground and Horacio had placed his foot where the bullet struck.

I asked him what had happened to the horse, and Isaac told me that after Horacio had been carried into the house by his six daughters, he had looked at the horse for a while and then shot it. I took Isaac's rifle and sent him home.

Horacio Medina lost two toes from his right foot and twisted his back badly when he fell.

Upon leaving, I met Father Joseph, who had been summoned by Horacio's oldest daughter, Cecelia. He agreed that it would be best to settle this matter quickly, before it got out of hand. I have paid Filemon Rodríguez one dollar of village money to remove the dead horse with his tractor.

Late in the afternoon, Father Joseph came to my office, complaining of the wind and the mud that he thought was worse than he could remember and also of his age, which was far too advanced for all the walking he had done on this day. He told me that Benito had agreed to give Horacio ten lambs for the loss of his toes and also that when his son Isaac complained of this, Benito struck him sharply on the side of his head with his hand. Father Joseph said that he then walked back to town and presented this offer to Horacio, who by this time was in little pain and quite drunk. Horacio demanded twenty lambs for the loss of his toes and also that Isaac work ninety days without pay in his employ the coming summer. Father Joseph told me he ate a hurried lunch with Horacio's daughters and again walked the long distance to Benito's house. Benito, after staring silently at the sky for a long period of time, agreed to the *arrangement and swore that never again would he consider the purchase of a horse. I told Father Joseph that he had done well, and he breathed deeply and said that it was not easy being priest for so many.*

Upon leaving, Father Joseph said that he had missed my presence at mass the past two Sundays and that he hoped this would not continue.

A thick bank of clouds could be seen in the west, and now in the dark they have moved and half the sky is with-out stars.

MARCH 4:
Berna Ruiz came to my office this morning. She walked alone, and in her arms she carried the three santos I had years before given to her and her family. She told me that her husband, Eloy, who sells wood to many people in this village, had removed the santos from their home two weeks before, after Father Joseph had spoken out against such things, and placed them in the woodshed behind their house. There they had stood looking at the fields until this morning, when Berna decided that they should be returned to me. All three were wrapped in a small blanket, and when I took them from her, she told me to be watchful of the smallest

Lady, as she could be disruptive and troublesome and was in need of constant discipline. I told her that I would and asked about the health of her family. She told me that her mother, who is ninety-six years old, has continued to shrink and no longer has hair upon her head, and that without teeth her mother has become as if an infant.

I have brought these three santos to my house and placed them with the others. It has begun to snow, and from my house I cannot see the lights from the village.

MARCH 5:

Four inches of new snow fell in the night, and at dawn the wind began to blow. It is cold. At sunset I looked down at the village from the doorway of my office. I could see no one, only the smoke from the chimneys. Even the cows stand still with ice on their backs, as if frozen.

MARCH 7:

Although it has snowed now for three days, the wind continues to blow, and there is no more than six inches on the ground.

I have brought beans and flour to the family of Ramón Trujillo. He has been gone from this village for eighteen

days in search of work to the south. His wife, Crusita,
told me that she is not yet concerned. But beneath her eyes
are circles of darkness.

When Ramona told Juan Trujillo that she was
leaving Guadalupe, that what she wanted for her
life was not in this village, he did not speak but
turned away from her. When she spoke his name,
he would not face her but shook his head, and
Ramona realized then that he had always known
this would come.

She walked out of his house and stood for a moment outside where, two years before, he had placed
four white crosses in the ground. One bore the
name of the woman who was not his mother,
Crusita Trujillo, and on the others were the names
of Juan's half-brothers and half-sister. Inside the
house, Juan began to sing a song Ramona had never
heard before. As she walked away, his voice faded,
and she felt as though her life were becoming larger.

"Ramona," Rosa called from the front door,
"are you all right, mi hija?"

Ramona turned in her chair. "Yes," she said. The front of Rosa's apron was dusted with flour and red chile.

"I was thinking of you, hija."

"I'm fine, Grandmother."

"Can I get you some coffee?"

"I'll come and get some soon."

Rosa turned from the door. "Eee, Loretta," she said, "you never stop," and Ramona heard the sound of Martha's laughter.

MARCH 8:

Demecio Segura, a frail man of seventy years who lives with his nephew, Luis, walked to my office this afternoon. He told me it took him four hours to walk the distance, which is not far, and with each footstep, he said, a pain would touch the back of his neck and reach into his chest for his heart. I told him that he should not be out in such weather, which continues to be cold with snow. Demecio agreed but said he was in need of assistance in composing a letter to his daughter, Estancia, who lives fifty miles to the south, where the climate is less harsh. In this letter, Demecio told his daughter that his health has been poor and that Luis

cooks seldom and that when he does, it is always goat meat
and beans without chile that taste like nothing. He had me
write that his last will and testament is under his bed,
where there is a cold draft from the cracks in the wall. It is
also his desire to give his daughter his wife's wedding dress
and marriage shoes, which are small and red, and also the
family Bible that has been passed down from his wife's
grandfather. These things are kept in a trunk which Luis,
who has no respect, uses as a chair at the kitchen table. He
wished for me to add that he misses the company of his
daughter and his grandchildren greatly and that he would
consider living in her home, where orchards of fruit trees
grow in the summer and where an old man would be less
likely to slip on the ice and hurt his bones in the winter
months. When this letter was completed, Demecio thanked
me, placed the paper inside his coat, and returned to his home.

MARCH 9:

On leaving my office this afternoon, I met Rosa Montoya,
who was returning home with her son, Lito. Lito no longer
wears the bandage on his forehead, and on his face below his
hat is a dark bruise. As we were not far from their home,

Rosa placed her hand on her son's shoulder and told him to walk ahead. He did not speak but did as she said. He walked slowly away from us, and with his head bent and his body hunched under the bulk of his coat, there was the feeling of age on this boy. Rosa told me that although Lito has recovered from his fall, she worries more about him now than before. She said that he has changed, as if a part of him has left, and what remains now carries a great weight. It was as though she'd had two sons, and now one of them was gone. I did not speak, and we stood and watched Lito make his way across the snow. When I looked at Rosa, she said with her face still toward Lito that the Lady I had given her stands against the wall in her bedroom and that the dreams she had been dreaming have ceased. She turned her face toward me and said that for all the cold and the snow of this winter, there have also been too many fires. She told me that at night Father Joseph has been burning the santos brought to the church by those who had them. I only looked back at her, and at that moment, for the first day of many, the sun could be seen in the west between the clouds and the mountains, and it made the snow that was falling look like embers.

Ramona looked up from the book, and her eyes came to rest on the old village office. She faintly remembered a time when the building was in use, when the field it sat in was kept mowed and vehicles were parked in the dirt drive before it. That was all she remembered. She couldn't ever remember being inside or even when it had outlived its usefulness. The sun was directly above her now, and she could feel the heat on the back of her neck. Behind her, inside her house, she could hear the low hum of voices and every so often the clatter of a pan. If she were to stand and walk over to the old building, she thought, her feet would pass over the same path that Lito, her father, had once taken on his way to school.

The door to the village office was ajar, and when Ramona pushed it with her shoulder, the bottom scraped roughly against the floor. She looked into the room from outside.

There was one small window, but it was so streaked and layered with cobwebs that it seemed to make the room even darker. She found a light switch dug into the adobe next to the door frame, and the room filled with a dim yellow light. The lightbulb hung naked from the ceiling in the middle of the room, and Ramona could see how badly the vigas sagged from years of snowloads. The wood was stained gray and black. A crooked entranceway opposite her led into a small back room, but her eyes were not yet accustomed to the shadows. Stacked and piled against all the walls was what seemed to be decades of broken or dismantled junk. Shovels with broken handles, ax and pick heads cast in rust, coffee cans flowing over with bolts and old nails, parts from ancient engines slabbed thick with dirt and grease, and in one corner a faded pile of clothes, wet and rotted.

The room swam with things used up and lost, except in the very center. There by themselves sat an old cast-iron stove and, beside it, a small oak table and chair. Ramona could see layers of dust on the tabletop, cobwebs that wound through the legs of the chair. She held the book written in Antonio Montoya's hand against her chest and stepped inside, toward the table. Beneath the odor of damp and rotting wood, she could sense the scent of cedar and smoke.

When Ramona left the village of Guadalupe at the age of nineteen, she sat alone in the back of the large bus as it drove west through other villages that, to her, looked dismal and empty. In her bag she had packed a black dress belonging to her mother, which Ramona had never worn anywhere, a change of soft cotton underwear that was pure white, three hundred and twelve dollars in silver that made Ramona feel she was carrying something of great weight, and a new set of charcoal pencils. Ramona thought that with these things there was nothing she could not do.

Near the end of the bus ride, Ramona had fallen asleep and dreamed of her brothers. She dreamed that Flavio was alone, looking out the windows of their house and weeping quietly at the loss of their mother. Baby José, who only walked backward, was in this dream also. He was lost in the yard where her father split wood. His face was dirty, and in the dream Ramona saw through José's eyes that he could only see where he had been. When Ramona woke, she found that the bus had arrived at her destination, and her dream flowed through her veins as if her blood had become thick and black.

Five weeks later, Ramona Montoya sat in her small rented house. It had once been a garage, and the four walls were painted yellow and smelled of exhaust fumes. In the yard outside grew one citrus tree that bore a strange red fruit that not even the birds ate. Ramona sat on the edge of her bed with her hands clenched in her lap and fought an almost overwhelming desire to return to Guadalupe and to her family. She reminded herself that she had, in fact, found a job, and although it involved cleaning floors for many hours a day, it was still a job she had found. And if her drawing was going poorly, and it was, she told herself she could work at it until it improved. Ramona lay back on the bed and stared at the ceiling. She wondered what kind of fruit it was that a bird wouldn't eat. She thought that just a mile from where she lived was a bus station, and if she were to walk there and purchase a ticket, she would be home with her family by the next day.

At some point, Ramona realized that she must have dozed off, for she became aware of someone walking away from her door. When she opened it, she found in her mailbox the only letter she was ever to receive from her grandmother. It read:

Dear Ramona,

I miss you so very much, mi hija. The nights are becoming cool, and your grandfather keeps busy as always. Your brothers Flavio and José are both well, as is your father. I write you to say that I am very proud you are my granddaughter, and I hope you are happy there. I am sending you something I found that your father made when he was a small boy. Do not forget to eat well and pray for me sometimes. My love to you always,

your grandmother

Ramona unfolded the piece of paper that was enclosed in the envelope. It was a sheet of gray-lined paper from a tablet, and on it was drawn in pencil hundreds of fish, and all of them had legs and small feet, and some were in trees and some were walking in fields of alfalfa.

Ramona lived away from Guadalupe for thirteen years and made a life for herself in a place where water ran hidden in culverts beneath the streets, and where chickens did not talk, and where the earth was covered with concrete and there was no such thing as mud. Seldom did Guadalupe enter her mind, but when it did, it was as if a hand had reached out and stroked her. Sometimes, and it seemed to be always at dawn, she would be riding the bus and would see the form of a man on the sidewalk, his shoulders hunched, his cap pulled low, and then she would see him in a field with a shovel, moving water with steel and wood. Or the wind would blow at night against her house, and Ramona would see hills of piñon and juniper, and there would be the sound of the wind rushing through the branches. One evening, lightning struck and the power went off, taking away the lights of the city. Ramona walked outside and, with her neighbors, looked at the sky, and there were only stars. Guadalupe became a scent that came only occasionally, but when it did, it was as if her bones could sense it.

There were men in her life, enough that Ramona gradually became aware of what each one desired of her. She practiced love with the conviction that she would eventually get it right. Sometimes, when unable to sleep, she would sit beside the bed and watch, from the light coming in the window, her lover breathe. She understood that his breath came from his mouth like hers, and she would lean close to his face and feel the soft push of air on her skin. She would trace his hand with her fingers as if there were a secret she could find only in the dark. There was a part of Ramona that even she couldn't reach, as if it were either buried too deep or had been given to something else.

Now, as a summer afternoon passed by her, she sat at a small oak table that was covered with dust, the journal of Antonio Montoya in her lap. She thought that she knew this man, but she didn't know from where.

EIGHT

"Y‌OU LET THIS FIELD TURN to nothing," Epolito said. He moved a clod of dirt from the ditch, and Flavio watched the water spread and sink into the ground. "This field would grow alfalfa to my waist, and look at it now. Not enough hay for a rabbit."

"It's not mine, Grandfather," Flavio said. The two of them were in the field alone. José had run back to the house over an hour ago to bring them drinking water and had yet to return.

Epolito turned his head to Flavio. "It's your sister's," he said sharply. "Who is closer to you than her? Don't tell me it isn't your field. I'm not so old I have to listen to that."

All the time he had been irrigating with Epolito, Flavio felt as though he and little José were the same age. Whenever he opened a ditch, his grandfather would grunt and with his shovel would ever so slightly change the flow of water. In truth, Flavio didn't know why this should surprise him. His relationship with his grandfather had always been such. It was not Epolito's fault if little changed after death.

"Ramona and I have never been close," Flavio said softly, although he did not know if this were really true or just something he had come to believe.

"And whose fault is that?" Epolito said.

"Ramona was always your favorite." The words rushed out of Flavio's mouth. He felt his face flush and regretted that he had said such a thing to his grandfather.

Epolito stared at his grandson. Finally he said, "So? When Ramona was young she smelled like lilacs. You smelled like a cabrón, Flavio. Who would you choose to be your favorite? A lilac or a goat?" Flavio, who had never thought of himself as a goat but had always been fond of lilacs, looked away and chose to say nothing.

"You, Flavio," his grandfather went on, "have a good wife and a home and acres of land, and you have let your sister be alone with herself. And you tell me you have never been close like there is some sickness between you. Don't be stupid, Flavio. Besides, you are the only man in the Montoya family now. You are the one little José will look up to. There's no one else."

Flavio looked back at his grandfather. He could see that he was taller than Epolito and that the brim of his grandfather's hat was soaked with sweat. He thought that his grandfather must be thirsty. Epolito raised his shovel and poked his grandson in the belly with the handle. "Are you listening, hijo?" he said.

Flavio looked past Epolito at the field. He could see that the alfalfa was no higher than his ankle. "It is too late this year for this field," Flavio said. "But next spring as soon as the snow is gone."

"Next spring," Epolito said. "And by summer the alfalfa will be as high as my shoulder."

"Yes," Flavio said.

They left their shovels spaded in the ground next to the ditch and walked back toward the house. After walking for a while with only the sound of Epolito's breath, Flavio said, "Grandfather, how did you and Grandmother come back?"

"Back from where?"

Flavio started to say, "From the dead," but he thought such words might sound harsh when spoken aloud. "Back from the afterlife," he said.

Epolito grunted. "You think I have not been here all this time?"

"Here?" Flavio said, and suddenly in his mind he saw Ramona eating and sleeping and working on her paintings, and all the time their grandparents in the house with her.

"You've been here all these years?" Flavio said. "You never left?"

"Sometimes your grandmother and I would walk to your house and visit you."

Flavio looked down at the ground. He pictured his grandparents standing outside his house at night, looking in the windows. He thought this would not be something he would tell Martha and then wondered if this were a common thing after death. Were all the houses in Guadalupe surrounded by ghosts staring in their relative's windows?

"But what of God?" Flavio said, and he spoke the words softly.

Epolito stopped walking. He looked at his grandson. "There are some things, hijo," he said, "that not even I know."

Flavio could hear the noise coming from Ramona's house while he was still fifty yards from the door. When he followed his grandfather into the kitchen, he saw that the room, which was normally still and empty, was jammed full of people. There was a party in Ramona's house, but in all of it his sister was nowhere to be seen.

Martha was sitting at the kitchen table, placing corn tortillas and chile in an enormous flat pan. Her face was damp and flushed from the heat, and when Flavio stopped in the entranceway, she glanced up and smiled almost wildly at him. Martha was nearly delirious with happiness. Grandmother Rosa was standing behind Martha, and when she saw Flavio, she too smiled and then bent over his wife's shoulder and whispered in her ear. Little José was sitting on the floor at the other end of the room with one leg crossed over the other, eating from a pile of corn chips stacked on his lap. Loretta, whom Flavio hadn't seen since the day she lay in her casket with her hands folded over her breasts and wearing a smile not her own, was at the sink washing dishes. When she saw Flavio, she rushed to him, and, putting her wet hands on both his cheeks, kissed him lightly on the lower lip.

"Flavio," she said, and Flavio could smell the scent of oranges on her breath. "Close your mouth, Flavio. It's open too much."

Beyond Loretta in the center of the room stood an old man who had no hair but only fuzz on the top of his head and whose large ears framed a face that was all bone and flesh that sunk inward. The clothes he wore hung on his body, and he supported himself with a cane in each hand. For a moment, Flavio thought that another dead relative had come to visit. Then he recognized that the old man was Alfonso Vigil, a friend of his grandfather's, who was over one hundred years old and naturally would not look his best. Shrill trumpets and guitars played loudly from a small radio on the counter above José's head, and Flavio saw that Alfonso was shuffling his feet slowly in a circle. The only other person in Ramona's kitchen sat at the table across from Martha, and he too was an old man, over the age of eighty years. He was Albert Vigil, Alfonso's eldest son, and his face was the color of ashes. Loretta patted Flavio's cheek. "That's better," she said. "Now sit down and I'll bring you a beer."

Flavio sat next to Albert, who did not even move his eyes toward him. Flavio looked across the table at his wife.

"We're cooking, Flavio," she said loudly, over the sound of the music.

"Yes," Flavio said.

"You look so good, mi hijo," Rosa said. "Did I tell you?"

"Yes, Grandmother," Flavio said. Loretta put a beer before him on the table, and Flavio watched her walk back to the sink.

"Flavio," Albert said. His serious voice wavered and cracked. "My father is dancing."

Flavio looked at Albert's father, who stared at the floor as he moved his feet. Alfonso's hands were curled tightly around the top of each cane like knots of a piñon stump.

"Yes," Flavio said. "Your father has always danced, Albert."

Albert moved his hand and placed it over Flavio's. "Are we all dead, Flavio?" he said.

Flavio thought that if he looked at Albert and his father together, they would look like brothers who had cheated death and were slowly becoming petrified. "No, Albert," he said. "The dead have only come to visit."

"Are you sure?"

"I think so." But Flavio felt a snag of doubt and wondered for a moment exactly who had crossed over to where. "Do you want a beer, Albert?"

Albert shook his head. "I have had my kidneys removed," Albert said. Flavio could see that Albert's left eye was glazed with cataracts and that when he spoke his teeth resembled teeth a horse would have. Albert leaned a little closer to Flavio. "Why are they here?"

Flavio shook his head. "I don't know, Albert," he said. "Maybe they are lonely." He felt Albert's hand tug at his own.

"Flavio," Albert said, "I would drink a little whiskey."

MARCH 10:
*It has snowed now for six days, and the cold is the
cold of January. This morning I walked to the church,
which is down the hill from the village office in a large
clearing where the land is flat. Father Joseph was not there,
and Modesta Griego, who has taken care of Father Joseph's
needs since I was a child, told me he had gone to visit
Horacio Medina, whose foot has become badly infected and
is twice its normal size and no longer resembles a foot.
Modesta, who is bent severely in the shoulders and speaks
only in a harsh whisper, said that Father Joseph has
been feeling poorly of late but that she would tell him I
had come.*

Upon leaving, I walked to the east side of the church, where the wall has swelled out badly through the years and is in need of buttressing. At the base of a large cottonwood that shades the church in the summer, I saw a large circle where there was no snow, only charred wood many inches thick. In the center of this circle the wood still smoked, and I could see a carved hand that was now black and the fingers bent in a way I could not recall making. I moved this from the embers and covered it with snow until it no longer burned, and at the tip of one finger I could see where the paint was still the color of flesh.

I waited until after dark for Father Joseph, and he did not appear. Still it snows this evening. It does not fall heavily and is, after so many days, no higher than my knee, but it snows steadily as though it will never stop.

MARCH 11:

Eduardo Muñoz, who is sixty-two years old and lives with his parents, came to my office on this day. He is a man who speaks seldom, and his mind is like that of a small child. His face was red from the cold, and he wore a hat that covered his ears and a coat that was too tight for his

body. When I asked him to come in and sit by the stove,
he shook his head and looked away. After a moment,
he said that he could not stay long, as his mother and
father often worry if he is away too long. I asked what
had brought him to my office, and he said he had come
to ask when the snow would stop. He was tired of this
weather and would like it to change. After this, Eduardo
looked down at his boots, which were soaked through, and
said nothing. When I asked him about the health of his
three sisters, who are all married and live close to their
parents' home, he told me they were also tired of the snow
and were increasingly irritable with each passing day.
I then told Eduardo that I believed the snow would
end soon as would the cold and that when the weather
broke, the air would be warm and he would see how green
the fields would become with so much moisture. Eduardo
thanked me and said nothing more. I watched him walk
quickly back down the hill. As he walked, his feet did not
rise above the snow.

MARCH 12:
Although the sky was thick with gray clouds today, there
was no snow, and in the evening stars could be seen.

MARCH 13:

Berna Ruiz came to my house just before dawn. Upon her head and falling down her back was a black shawl, and she told me that in the night her mother had died. She went on to say that her family was now asleep, as was Father Joseph, who had spent the night at her mother's bedside. The sky beyond Berna was full of stars that I had not seen for many days, and there was no wind. I told her I was sorry to hear such news but that her mother had lived many years and that it was good that Father Joseph had been present. Berna said that in the final hour, her mother had lain with her eyes wide open, and when she breathed, she made the sound of a small bird. We did not speak for some time, and when I asked Berna what I could do, she said that she had come to my house to ask my permission to speak with the Lady she had returned just days ago. I could see the thin lines of blood in her eyes and the deep creases at the corners of her mouth. She remained for more than an hour with the Lady, while I sat by the stove and listened to the sound of Berna's voice, which came soft and muffled from the other room. Berna thanked me as she left my house. When I entered the room she had been in, I found that the santo who had once worn a towel over her head now had a moist handkerchief covering her feet. In her hands was a strand of hair that was white and fine. I have let these things remain where Berna left them.

In the afternoon, the temperature rose well above freezing, and there is the sound of running water beneath the snow.

MARCH 15:

Today Father Joseph walked to my office. There was a look of fatigue about him, and his face, which has always been full and red, is now drawn and with a slight cast of yellow. He told me that the infection in Horacio Medina's foot, which had been severe, has subsided, although he has lost another toe which turned black and dry and fell off almost by itself. He told me also that he had been present at the death of Florilla Martínez, the mother of Berna Ruiz, and that when she had breathed her last, a sound like a bird had come from her mouth, and her arms and legs had trembled as if she had thought to fly. He added that this had disturbed his sleep the past two evenings, as he felt that humans near death should fall gracefully into the arms of God, not *suddenly bear the countenance of animals. We did not speak for some moments, and Father Joseph, for the first time since entering my office, raised his eyes and asked what it was I wished to speak with him about. I told him that I had heard he was burning santos outside the church and also that when I had walked there I had seen where this had been done. We were silent for some time, and beneath Father Joseph's eyes I could see circles of darkness. Finally he said that what I had heard was true and that he had burned more than thirty santos. At this, he rose with some effort from his chair and walked to the door. He said he had known me since I was a child, and he was sorry for what had come to pass. He said at his age there is an understanding that some things come to an end, and although it is painful, that too will pass. He added that, having given his life to God and the church, he must follow their wishes. Or what, he asked, would he possess then?*

In my house, in the room that has no window, remain the five santos and also the one on which I no longer work.

MARCH 16:
My sister, who was christened Ramona Montoya and was my only sibling, died on this day twenty-one years ago at

the age of twelve. She is buried in the Guadalupe cemetery that sits on a small hill and lies in a coffin made of rough pine that my father and I made the afternoon of her death. As that spring was warm and dry, we were able to dig a deep grave so that my sister lies beneath many feet of dirt. Six months after her death and soon after our mother left us, my father, who had always been a strong man, stopped eating in much the same way an infant will. Within a month he was confined to bed, and one morning he did not wake. When my sister died, she took with her the mind and soul of my mother and she also took with her my father.

The sun was now shining through the door of the office, and its light spread across the floor and onto the table in the center of the room where Ramona sat reading. She could feel tightness in the back of her neck. In the sunlight, she could see motes of dust that floated without falling, and she knew that, although she had read only a few pages, the sun was now low in the west and hours had passed. Ramona was beginning to feel as if she were living in two places and that she was losing time and herself in both. She rose from the chair and then for no reason reached down and flipped over a number of pages in the open book. She turned to an entry dated June 2. It read, "Juanito Griego, son of Juan and Estelle Griego, drowned in an irrigation ditch that runs behind their house. Juanito's sister, Victoria, said that he fell in and floated away too fast."

Ramona stared down at the journal and saw that the handwriting was not that of Antonio Montoya. The letters were printed large and awkwardly, the way a child would write in learning. Her hand was lying on the page, and Ramona could see how thin her fingers were and how her skin was dry and cracked. She turned a few more pages to September 23, and in the same print was written, "Tomás Rael's truck ran down the hill going into the village with no driver and killed a horse belonging to Martín Gonzáles." Ramona watched her hand turn all the pages in the book. "December 25: It is Christmas Day, and it is snowing."

For a moment, Ramona did nothing. She looked down at the words written by someone else. Then she flipped the pages back to the last entry she had read by Antonio Montoya. March 16. At some point between that day and the second of June, Antonio had ceased to speak. Ramona had no idea what that meant, nor what it meant to her. She walked to the entrance to the back room, and in the shadows against the far wall, she could see a large stack of books on the floor. She knelt before them and took one from the top. It was dated 1925. The cover was soft and wet, the pages stained. The first entry was written in the same awkward print as before. She reached for another book from other years, and then another, and in none of them could she find the writing of Antonio Montoya. When Ramona finally stopped, the books were spread about her, and she wondered just what it was she had lost.

When Ramona entered her house, the first thing she saw was Flavio sitting on her small couch and next to him, an old man whose head came only to Flavio's shoulder. Both were smiling at her as if awaiting her return, and on the lap of the old man were his false teeth and a bottle of whiskey that was three-quarters empty.

"Ramona," Flavio said, and Ramona could tell where much of the whiskey had gone. "Ramona, this is my friend Albert Vigil. He is the oldest son of Alfonso Vigil." Albert bobbed his head twice, and although he continued to smile, he did not speak. Ramona wondered how a man so old could be called the son of anyone. She watched Albert take a small sip of the whiskey and then pass the bottle to her brother.

"Ramona," Flavio said, "Albert has no kidneys."

"I have no liver, también," Albert said in a voice that sounded full of gravel. Flavio looked at Albert fondly in much the way a father would look at his son.

"Flavio," Ramona said, and Flavio looked back at her, "where is Grandmother?"

"She is in the kitchen," Flavio said. "Cleaning. Where have you been, Ramona? You have missed the party."

"I've been outside," Ramona said, and she saw that Flavio was no longer smiling and was looking at her in such a way that she thought he might once again begin to weep. "Flavio," she said, "are you all right?"

"Ramona," he said, and he held out his hand, "you have always smelled like lilacs, Ramona."

She stepped toward her brother and took his hand. She knelt down and said, "I think you have had a little too much whiskey, Flavio."

"I have," Flavio said. Beside him, Albert snaked out his arm and took the bottle from between Flavio's legs and stuck it tightly between his own.

"I am sorry for everything, Ramona," Flavio said. "I have been no brother, and the field is only weeds."

Ramona, who had no idea what her brother was talking about, could smell the heavy scent of whiskey coming from the two men and the flat odor of tobacco. She thought of her father and saw him as a child walking slowly across the snow with a white bandage on his forehead. She patted Flavio's hand gently.

"Did you know, Flavio," she heard herself say, "that our father as a boy drew pictures of fish with legs and one day leaped from the small attic of this house and hurt himself severely? This happened during a terrible winter, and for days he wore a bandage across his forehead."

Flavio looked down at his sister. He knew that he had drunk too much whiskey, and it was possibly because of this that he did not know how this conversation with his sister had suddenly turned to their father, whom Flavio thought of seldom and never as a child. In his mind, he saw his father as he always had, with his shoulders, which were broad and heavy, dipped toward the ground and his head slightly bent. He remembered that their father spoke little and seemed to be out of place in their house.

"Your father did not do well here," Albert said. "I knew him all his life."

Both Ramona and Flavio turned to look at Albert. Ramona could see that Albert's left eye was the color of milk and that without his teeth the flesh on his cheek sagged. "He did not do well where?" Ramona asked.

"Here," Albert said, and he moved one of his feet slightly. "He did not do well with life. It was difficult for him."

"Where did my father want to be?" Flavio asked.

Albert shrugged his thin shoulders. "Elsewhere," he said. "Nowhere," and he lowered his eyes. "Flavio," he said, "my teeth are in my lap."

"Yes, Albert," Flavio said. "You put them there."

"Why?"

"I don't know," Flavio said. He turned and looked at Ramona, who could see the redness in his eyes. "Ramona," he said, "we are all that is left of our family."

And Ramona, who had never once considered this, said, "We are," and she could feel how warm her brother's hand was in hers, and again she saw her father make his way slowly across the snow.

NINE

W HEN RAMONA WALKED INTO the kitchen, her grandmother was standing at the sink, and although her hands were in the dishwater, she was standing motionless and staring out the small window. Epolito was sitting at the kitchen table, and across from him sat Alfonso Vigil. Ramona had not seen him since she was a child and only recognized him because of his large ears, which seemed to have grown larger over the years while the rest of his body had not. Her grandfather glanced at her and then looked back at Alfonso. Epolito spoke in a low voice. "We have been left behind, Alfonso. It is not like when we were young. There is nothing of importance now. Then, the alfalfa would grow to your waist."

Ramona walked across the room to the sink. "Grandmother," she said.

Rosa Montoya turned and looked at Ramona. "Hija," she said in a voice that made Ramona think that her grandmother had been somewhere far away.

"Grandmother, why am I reading this book?"

"That is the journal Antonio Montoya wrote," Rosa said.

"Yes, I know that, Grandmother. But why am I reading it?"

"You need me to tell you that?"

"Grandmother," Ramona said, "please."

"It is something you needed to know, Ramona. It is a story of this village."

"It is more than that, Grandmother. What happened to the man who wrote these things?"

Rosa turned and looked at her granddaughter. "Where have you been all this time, Ramona?" she said softly. "Your face is full of dirt."

"I've been in the village office."

"Everyone was here, hija. We had a feast. I tell you to sit outside in the sun for a little while, and you come back hours later."

Ramona closed her eyes. She felt like shaking this old woman who was tormenting her. "Grandmother," she said.

"There is food in the refrigerator, Ramona. I want you to eat now."

For a moment, neither woman spoke. "The sun is setting, Ramona," Rosa said. "I wish to do the dishes quietly. Go wash and come and eat. Later we will talk."

In the other room Ramona saw that her brother and Albert had fallen asleep on the couch and that Albert's teeth had fallen to the floor but the whiskey bottle was still stuck firmly between his legs. In the bathroom, she washed the dirt from her face and hands, and when she returned to the kitchen, a place was set at the table for her.

Rosa, who was still at the sink, said without turning, "Sit, Ramona, and keep your grandfather company. You remember Alfonso Vigil." Raising her voice, Rosa said, "This is mi hija, Alfonso. You remember."

Alfonso raised his bleary eyes and looked at Ramona. Then he said something that Ramona did not understand.

"Yes," her grandmother said from the sink, "she has grown. She is the oldest of my grandchildren."

"Where is your brother?" Epolito said.

"He's in the other room," Ramona said, and she sat down at the end of the table. "He is napping."

Epolito grunted. "Napping," he said. "He and your son," and here Epolito looked across the table at Alfonso, "have done nothing but drink whiskey. They will nap all night."

"Where is little José?" Ramona asked. "Where have Loretta and Martha gone?"

"How should I know?" Epolito said. "At least they're not drinking whiskey."

"They have gone for a little walk, hija," Rosa said. "Not too far, I don't think."

Ramona could smell the cilantro on her plate. She took a bite and realized she was starving. Alfonso again turned his head to look at Ramona.

He spoke in such a whisper that Ramona heard
nothing.

"He asked," Epolito said, "if you still draw
people of this village naked?"

Ramona, who had not blushed for a great many
years, felt her face grow warm. She wondered how
it was that so many things she had always thought
were hers alone seemed to be known by so many.
Without looking at Alfonso, she said, "No, I do
not do that anymore."

"I'm glad to hear that, hija," Rosa said from
the sink.

"Alfonso says," Epolito said, "that he has never
wished to see what is beneath his neighbor's
clothing."

The kitchen fell silent but for the sound of
water in the sink and the soft noise of Ramona's
fork against the plate.

"He says," Epolito said, although again Ramona
had not heard Alfonso speak, "that he has outlived
almost all of his children and his children's wives
and three of his grandchildren. That of his children

only Albert remains. He says that it is not bad to be old but that it is not so good to become too old."

Alfonso's head was bent and was but inches from the table top. She remembered him as a younger man who, in the evenings, would sit outside with her grandfather and talk and sometimes, if they drank, would dance in small circles. She realized that even so long ago, she had thought of this man as old.

"He has much to be proud of," Ramona said, and when Epolito said this to Alfonso, Ramona watched him nod his head in much the same way Albert had.

Ramona finished eating and rose from the table and brought her plate to the sink. "Grandmother," she said.

"As a young woman, Ramona," Rosa said, "I stood in this same place before this same window. So many years." She turned and looked at Ramona. "All my life, I think."

"Yes," Ramona said.

"Come, hija. We'll sit outside where we won't disturb your grandfather."

Ramona followed her grandmother from the kitchen and stood beside her when she stopped before Flavio and Albert, who were both still asleep. "When your grandfather was a young man, Ramona, he looked much like Flavio. He was so handsome and so strong."

Flavio's mouth hung open, and he was snoring gently. His head hung awkwardly to one side. Rosa walked to the bedroom and came out carrying a heavy blanket, which she laid over the two sleeping men. "There, mi hijo," she said softly, and Ramona thought that her brother and Albert would swelter beneath the quilt.

Rosa sat in the wicker chair beneath the cottonwood, and Ramona sat not far from her in the grass. The sun had set, and only the tops of the mountains to the east caught sunlight. Rosa looked at her granddaughter.

"Did you know, Ramona, that when your father married your mother, we held such a party here in this very place that the whole village of

Guadalupe came? The cooking. And the dancing.
And the children who ran everywhere. It was a
joyful day, and the weather was like a crystal. Your
father was so happy on that day, Ramona, and
your mother, who always had a sadness about her,
sat under this same tree, and her face shone like
the sun." Rosa stopped talking. She smiled and
looked down at Ramona. "You have things to ask
of me, hija?"

Ramona suddenly thought that to sit in the
grass with this woman was enough. She turned
her head and looked across the road at the village
office. She saw how there were weeds growing
from the adobe where the plaster had fallen
away from one wall. She looked back at her
grandmother.

"What happened to the man who wrote in the
journal?" she asked. "His writing stops, Grandmother. He is in none of the other books. What
happened to him?"

Rosa looked at her granddaughter. "He left this
village," she said. "He left just days before Easter
of that same year."

"You remember this?"

For a moment, Rosa did not speak. She moved her eyes away from Ramona and said, "Do you think I could forget?"

"Where did he go?"

"So many questions, hija," Rosa said. She moved her shoulders slightly. "I don't know the answer to that, Ramona. To another town. To another village; I don't know. He left one morning carrying a small bag, and I did not see him leave. He walked from his house and down the hill to the road, and he left this village. By chance, Eduardo Muñoz, who was a grown man but whose mind was that of a child, met Antonio on the road that morning. Eduardo had come to believe that it was Antonio Montoya who had put an end to that winter, and when they met on the road that morning, he thanked Antonio for this and then asked when the spring winds, which he said made his ears ache, would cease. Antonio replied that the wind would blow until the mud was gone and enough snow had melted that the ditches would run full. He told Eduardo that when this season passed, the alfalfa would grow like never before and the days would be warm and there would be the sound of running water everywhere. Eduardo was the last to see Antonio Montoya in this village."

"But why?" Ramona said. "Why did he leave?"

Rosa opened and then closed her mouth. After a moment, she said, "He did not leave this village, hija. This village left him." Rosa turned her eyes back to Ramona. "It took from him everything, and then it left him alone. And so . . . "

Ramona did not speak but only looked at her grandmother until Rosa turned her face away. "You wish there to be an end to this story, hija," she said. "But there is no end. It is like everything else. I do not know what happened to the life of Antonio Montoya. He left our lives, and we became full of other things."

A slight breeze moved the leaves of the cotton-wood. Rosa closed her eyes. "I can smell the wind, hija," she said. "It smells of garlic and smoke. Do you have more questions to ask?"

"Yes," Ramona said, although she no longer knew what they were.

"I have a favor to ask of you," Rosa said with her eyes still closed, "before you ask me these things."

"What is it, grandmother?"

"I wish you to read to me. From the journal. Will you do that, mi hija?"

"Yes."

MARCH 18:
There has been no freeze in the night for the past two days. The snow in this village is gone, and there is only mud that is everywhere. For the first time in months, I heard the sound of sheep in my neighbor's field. I think the winter has finally left us.

"That was a bad winter," Rosa said. She was sitting straight in the wicker chair with her hands in her lap. "So many were sick. And the snow and the cold. That was the winter your father climbed into the small space above the ceiling of this house and leaped, as if he could fly, into the snow and struck his head, and when fires burned in the cemetery for days upon days, and the sky above it was black with smoke. You never saw such a thing, Ramona. The earth was like stone."

It seemed to Ramona that for a winter that had been so long and so cold, it had also been full of flames, and then she remembered that her grandmother as a young woman had said the same thing to Antonio Montoya.

"The priest," Ramona said, "burned the santos."

Rosa Montoya opened her eyes. "Father Joseph," she said. "Yes. He did that. He burned them at night beside the church. It was a hard time, hija."

"And what of your dreams?"

"My dreams passed, hija. Read."

MARCH 19:
Today Demecio Segura walked to my office. He complained of the condition of the road, and his trousers were wet with mud far above his boots. He had come to my office once again to thank me for composing the letter he had sent to his daughter, who lives a number of miles south of this village. In a few days he is to leave Guadalupe and begin

to live the remainder of his life where already the orchards are in bloom.

"Eee, that man," Rosa said. "He never had any luck that was good. His wife, who was of the García family, died in her midlife when she fell from a tree while gathering piñon. Imagine, a woman that old climbing trees. And then to fall. After his daughter, Estancia, ran away to marry a man no one knew anything about, Demecio moved in with his nephew, Luis, who did not speak in words but only grunted and later came to a bad end himself. No wonder Demecio wished to leave this village. Later that same spring, while fishing near his daughter's home, he was drowned when the river overflowed its bank and carried him away as if he were a stick."

. . . I told him I would be sorry to see him leave this village where he has lived his whole life, but that it is good to be near one's family. He agreed and told me he plans to do nothing with his remaining years but enjoy the apples his daughter grows and fish in the river near his daughter's house.

MARCH 23:

I have spoken with no one for a number of days. The wind blows hard in the afternoon, and the days have become longer. In the evenings and the early mornings, smoke rises from along the irrigation ditches where some have begun to burn away the weeds and debris.

MARCH 25:

On the evening of this day, Epolito Montoya, who is my first cousin and the husband of Rosa Montoya . . .

Here, Ramona stopped reading. Suddenly she did not want to know what was written in the journal. She felt as though she were gazing into the soul of things that had been hidden for a long time.

"It is too dark to read, Grandmother," she said.

Rosa opened her eyes and smiled. "You cannot see the words?" she asked.

"Barely."

"There is only a little left, hija."

. . . came to my house. In his arms, he carried the Lady that I had given to Rosa and that bears the name of my sister. Finally he said that he and Rosa were grateful that I had

allowed the Lady to stay in their home but that they could keep it no longer. I told him I understood and then asked of Rosa's dreams. He told me that she has been sleeping well and dreamless and that he hoped this would continue. When I asked him about Lito, he said that his son has improved but continues to be quiet and keeps to himself much of the time. He said that in the next few days, he will board up and nail shut the attic space from where Lito jumped so that no one ever again climbs up there. There was a silence after these words that weighed heavily on us both, and then Epolito wished me good-night and left.

MARCH 26:

This morning, Melquiades Cortéz was found dead by his neighbor, Pablo Quintana. Pablo told me that since the day Melquiades gave up his children to the care of his brother, he has been visiting Melquiades daily, if only for a short period of time. On this morning, he found Melquiades lying as if asleep outside his house. Beneath him upon the ground was only a thin blanket, and his body was naked to the weather. Pablo said that the face and skin of Melquiades Cortéz were the color of chalk and were like ice to the touch, and his body was curled like an infant's.

Melquiades Cortéz, who was thirty-four years old and the father of four children, is to be buried beside his wife in the Guadalupe cemetery.

Ramona stopped reading and looked up at her grandmother. Rosa was sitting with her eyes closed, and there was a slackness about her face. Her chest rose and fell slowly. "Grandmother," Ramona said, and after a moment Rosa moved her lips without speaking. Ramona looked back down at the journal. In the fading light she could barely make out the words.

MARCH 29:
This morning, I watched Rosa Montoya walk her son, Lito, to school. Although we did not speak and I saw her face only briefly, I could see fatigue around her eyes and that she looked only at the ground as she walked.

APRIL 1:
From the door of my office this morning, I watched Father Joseph walk from the church and up the hill to this office. Before he had come halfway, he stopped and looked toward

me. He did not call out or raise his hand, and after some moments he turned and walked back to the church.

APRIL 7:

I have spoken with no one for days. I write this in my journal, which is the journal of this village and which will remain here. Tomorrow I will leave Guadalupe, where my father and my sister are buried. I have brought the santos that are in my care to the village office and will leave them here for Father Joseph. They have stood in my house as if alone in the world and of no use, and I can no longer bear their presence.

It has begun to snow, and the flakes are heavy and fall slowly. In the sky there are no clouds, but stars and snow are everywhere.

Ramona turned the page, and there was nothing. The page was blank. She turned it and then another, and she realized that there was no more to read. Antonio Montoya's journal had ended. Ramona heard as if from far away her grandmother's voice.

"Hija," Rosa said in a whisper, "help me to the house."

Ramona put the book down in the grass, and she stood and took her grandmother's arm. "Are you all right, Grandmother?" she said.

"Yes," Rosa said. "It has been a long day, hija, and I'm tired. If I lie down for a little while. . . ."

Ramona helped her to her feet, and the two of them walked slowly to the house. It was almost completely dark now, and no light was lit inside the house. As they approached the front door, it swung open and Alfonso Vigil and his son, Albert, came out, leaning against each other as they walked, and Ramona noticed that they were the same height. She could hear the squeak of the rubber tips of Alfonso's canes as they slid a little on the front porch. As they passed Ramona and her grandmother, Rosa reached out and touched Alfonso's arm. Alfonso nodded, but neither spoke as they walked by, and Ramona thought it was as if she and her grandmother were not there.

The first thing Ramona saw when she entered the house was that her brother was no longer on the couch, and the blanket that had covered Flavio and Albert was lying on the floor.

"Flavio," Ramona said in the darkness, and she thought that her voice sounded loud and that her home had become enormous and empty.

"He's gone, hija," Rosa said.

"He's gone where?"

"Home. He and Martha have gone home."

"But his truck is still here, Grandmother."

"He has left, Ramona," Rosa said again.

Ramona could no longer see her grandmother's face. "Why is this house so quiet?" she asked, and then she called José's name.

Ramona felt her grandmother's hand tighten on her arm. "He's with his mother, hija," Rosa said, and suddenly Ramona felt a soft wave of panic.

"Tell me where they've gone, Grandmother," Ramona said, and even in her own ears, her voice sounded harsh.

"Help me to my bed, hija," her grandmother said.

Ramona helped her grandmother lie down and then sat on the bed beside her. "Grandmother," she said, "tell me."

"I'm going to rest now for a little while. And then maybe we can talk more, Ramona." Rosa folded her hands together on her chest. As Ramona rose from the bed, her grandmother said, "Cuidado, mi hija. Please."

"Careful of what, Grandmother?" she asked, but Rosa Montoya did not answer.

Ramona went into the kitchen and switched on the light. The room was empty. Everything was in its place, the dishes put away, the floor swept, a dishtowel folded by the sink. She thought that it looked exactly as it always had, as if nothing had changed. "Where is José?" Ramona spoke the words aloud.

She walked back through the house to the front door and stepped out into the August night to call him. She walked down the steps and away from the house, and about her was a coldness, and falling from the sky was snow.

T E N

RAMONA FELT THE SNOW turn to water on her bare arms, and when she looked up she could see only stars through the snow. In that second, she knew she was lost, and she felt in her soul that she would remain so and that there was no longer a path leading to where she had come. She turned back around quickly with the thought that she should escape back into the house, and in the window she saw the face of a woman staring out at her. She could see the youth in this woman's face and the paleness of her features and how her black hair was undone from its braids and fell in shadows past her shoulders. Their eyes met, as if spanning a great distance. Ramona said her grandmother's name and knew that the house before her, which had once been hers, was now truly her grandparents', and in it there was not a place for her.

Ramona turned and stepped toward the road, and she stumbled slightly over the ridges of frozen mud beneath her feet. Across the road through the snow she could see the village office, and from the one small window a yellow light was burning. On the road, which was no more than ruts, the shadow of a man walked toward her, and as he neared she heard him speak her name in a voice she knew. He drew closer and stood before her, and she saw how tired his eyes looked. His hands were in his pockets, and his shoulders slumped.

"Ramona," he said. "What are you doing here, Ramona?"

Ramona opened her mouth, her throat and chest so knotted that she thought she would never be able to speak. "José," she said, and she reached out to touch her brother's face.

"I can't stay, Ramona," he said, and he smiled a little. Ramona could see the white, straight edge of his teeth. "I'm almost there."

"José," Ramona said again. "I'm so glad to see you, José," and she rested her hand on the side of his face.

José took his hands from his pockets. He took his sister's hand in his. "Did you know, Ramona, that our grandfather's great-great-grandfather came to this village when there was nothing here but a few poor houses, and with his hands he built the church, and it took him years, and when he was done, he named it the Church of Our Lady of Guadalupe?"

"No, José," Ramona said, and she held on to his hand tightly. "I didn't know that."

"I've seen so much," he said, and he squeezed her hand hard. "I have to go. It's just a little further."

"José," Ramona said.

"I have a favor to ask you," José said. "If you ever in your life see a cow on the highway, my .22 is under my bed. Have little José shoot it for me." He let go of his sister's hand.

"José," Ramona said, "stay with me. I'm lost here, José."

As he walked backward away from her, her brother said, "You were never lost, Ramona. Tell my son that I love him."

When Antonio Montoya opened the door of the village office, standing before him was a woman he had never seen before. She wore no coat, and her arms were bare. Her hair was damp and fell to her shoulders. Beyond her, he could see that the snow was still falling and there was no wind, and when the snow touched the ground, it turned to water. When he brought his eyes back to this woman, she was staring as if she knew him, and for a moment both stood in silence with only the sound of the fire in the stove. Then he asked her what it was he could do. She did not answer, and in her face Antonio Montoya could see that the line of her mouth and the darkness of her eyes were things he had seen before, but he did not know where. He asked her name, and she closed her eyes and shook her head. In that moment, Antonio Montoya thought she would turn and leave, but she stepped still closer to him, and the light touched her arms and face. He asked again what he could do, and she spoke for the first time aloud. In a low voice, she said that she had come to this place to ask a favor of him. She said that she knew him to be a santero. Antonio Montoya said nothing, and after a long moment, he stepped away from the door and Ramona walked into the room.

The light of the lamp shone with a yellow cast on the surface of the small table, and on the table was a book that was new and was open. Ramona walked to it and looked down and read the words "It has begun to snow, and the flakes are heavy and fall slowly. In the sky there are no clouds, but stars and snow are everywhere."

She raised her eyes and could see the rest of the room in shadows. The mud plaster on the walls was smooth and thick, without cracks, and the adobe floor was clean and shone dully in the light. The vigas overhead ran straight, without sag, and the wood was white with drops of pitch that were the color of gold.

Against the wall of the room where there was little light were the seven santos, one of which had been merely touched with the knife. They stood like children together, and their eyes were open and their hands at their breasts, and some were taller than others and none smiled, but there was a softness about their mouths. Ramona walked to them and knelt, and she touched each one as if she were blind, and she thought she might begin to speak aloud to these Ladies and that in their silence they would answer. She saw that one held strands of fine white hair in her hands, and at her feet was a piece of white cloth, and in the eyes of this one there was the hint of a smile, and of other things, and Ramona thought of Berna Ruiz and of her aged mother and how this Lady and two of the others had stood for weeks in a woodshed and looked out together over a field of snow.

Upon another she saw a stain in the bend of the right elbow, as if blood had flowed out from inside the arm. She saw the age in another and how the paint was faded and peeled upon her face and how there was a crack that ran through her body. On the tallest one, whose dress was painted the deep color of blood, Ramona ran her fingers down the arm to the wrist, and with her fingertips she felt the marks of her own name. She closed her eyes and thought she would fade away in this room and become no more than a shadow.

After a moment, Ramona rose and turned and faced Antonio Montoya, who had not moved from the door. In his face she saw and did not see the faces of her brothers, and her father and her grandfather, and also little José. She saw the Montoyas in his face, and in his eyes she saw her own. Behind her, Ramona could feel the gaze of the santos, and she told Antonio Montoya that she wished to take all of the Ladies. When he did not answer, she saw that he was looking not at her but at the figures which stood against the wall. When he looked at her once again, he asked only one thing, and that was her name. At this, Ramona walked across the room and stood so close to him that she could smell the odor of smoke on his mouth. She took his hand and brought it to her face and said that in the night she had dreamed, and in this dream, the cemetery of Guadalupe was on fire, and the flames came together like water and engulfed the grass and the weeds, and when the fire was spent, the crosses and the stones stood out white against the burnt earth.

———————

At dawn, which came pale and warm, Ramona stood outside her house, and she could see how twisted the window in her house was and how the paint had come away and that the wood frame beneath was gray with age. She saw that her house needed to be plastered or it would turn to dirt.

She walked up the front steps to the door and opened it and went inside her house. She walked through the living room to the spare room, and when she looked in, she saw that little José was sleeping on the cot and that he looked small beneath the blanket.

In her own bedroom, she sat gently on the bed beside her grandmother, who lay as pale and still as death. Ramona touched her grandmother's hair and then stroked her forehead. "Grandmother," she said.

Rosa opened her eyes. "Ramona," she said in a whisper, "you're back."

"Yes," Ramona said.

"And you weren't gone too long."

"No," Ramona said, although she felt as though she had been away an eternity.

Rosa reached for her granddaughter's hand and said, "We have had a pact all these years, mi hija. All my life, it seems."

"Yes, Grandmother," Ramona said.

"I have a favor to ask."

"Another?" Ramona asked, and smiled.

"Yes," she said, and was quiet for a moment. "Go to the window, hija, and tell me things."

Ramona rose from the bed and looked out the window at the still, sunless morning. "I can see the field from here, Grandmother, and the tracks of Grandfather and Flavio and little José's feet in the mud."

"Your hijo is such a good boy, Ramona," Rosa said softly from the bed.

"Yes," Ramona said, and she smiled again. "Beyond the field is sagebrush, and past that the foothills begin, and they're thick with piñon and juniper, and on the top is a wide grove of aspen whose leaves even so early in August are beginning to yellow. The sky, Grandmother, looks white without the sun, and there are no clouds. It will be a warm day without wind. A day to do anything."

Ramona stopped talking, and when she finally looked away from the window at the bed, it was empty. She walked from her bedroom to the room where José was sleeping. She pushed him to one side and then climbed into the cot beside him. She lay there with her arms around him, and the last thing she could recall before sleep was that this boy in her arms smelled like mud—and he would bathe first thing.

ELEVEN

"JOSÉ," RAMONA SAID, "I think you should leave those alone and eat."

José was sitting across from his aunt, and he was pushing Albert Vigil's false teeth around the surface of the table with his fork. "Tía," he said, "how do you forget your teeth?"

Ramona looked at José's plate and saw that he had eaten almost all of his food and that his glass of milk was empty. "You drink too much whiskey," she said. "That's how." José picked up the teeth, which were white and pink, and held them in his hand.

"How do these work?" he asked.

Ramona leaned back in her chair and folded her arms across her chest. She looked at the teeth in

José's hand. She thought that Albert would be eating soup. "You put glue on them and stick them in your mouth."

"They look like toy teeth," José said. "Like those teeth that talk."

"When Albert has them in his mouth, they talk."

José looked up at Ramona. "My mother is gone, isn't she, Tía?"

"Yes, José," Ramona said. "I think she is."

"She said she would turn to smoke."

"Yes." Ramona leaned across the table and took José's hand. "Like smoke, José. Now come with me. There's something I want to see."

There was an old wooden ladder behind the shed where Ramona kept her paintings, and she and José dragged it out from the weeds and stood it against the south side of the house. It was past noon, and the sun was high in the sky and hot, and there was no wind. Ramona could see how the trapdoor where her father had once climbed and leaped into the snow was nailed shut, and she could see the tracks of rust where the nails had bled for years upon years.

"What are we going to fix?" José said.

"Nothing," Ramona said. "We're going to open that door and see what's inside. Now run to my truck. In the back is a steel bar. Go get it and bring it here."

The wood was rotten, and the small trapdoor pried loose easily. Ramona swung open the door and could feel on her face the rush of warm air and the strands of spider webs that wove from the back of the door to the rafters inside. There was the smell of age and old dirt. José yelled something from below that Ramona did not hear. A few feet inside stood seven figures, layered in dust as if clothed in shrouds. They stood close together, and at the foot of one was a small piece of cloth that was no more than a rag. Ramona shut her eyes tightly, and she could feel the sun on the back of her neck.

She passed each one down to José, who stood them by the ladder in the sun, and to him these things looked like creatures that had come from a place far away. Ramona climbed down the ladder carrying the last Lady, which was the tallest. When Ramona stood her with the others, she thought that her life was so full it might explode.

Little José felt his Tía Ramona's hand come to rest on his shoulder. He looked at the unfinished santo that seemed more like wood than anything else, and he thought of the time his father had showed him how to carve a small crucifix out of wood. His father had said to him, "You carve, José, with the blade away from you always. And you take only a little away at a time. If you do that, mi hijo, you will see things in the wood that have been there forever."